P9-DUV-368

DATE DUE

DEMCO 38-296

MASTER OF THE
DAY OF JUDGMENT

MASTER OF THE DAY OF JUDGMENT

Leo Perutz

Translated from the German by
Eric Mosbacher

ARCADE PUBLISHING • NEW YORK

PT 2631 .E5 M413 1994

Perutz, Leo, 1882-1957.

Master of the day of
  judgment

                                          the title *Der Meister des*
Jüngsten Tages

The characters and events in this book are fictitious. Any similarity to real
persons, living or dead, is coincidental and not intended by the author.

Library of Congress Cataloging-in-Publication Data

Perutz, Leo, 1882–1957
    [Meister des jüngsten Tages. English]
    Master of the day of judgment / Leo Perutz ; translated from the
German by Eric Mosbacher. —1st North American ed.
        p.   cm.
    ISBN 1-55970-171-4
    I. Mosbacher, Eric, 1903–   . II. Title.
PT2631.E5M413   1994
833'.912—dc20   94-14353

Foreword instead of a Postscript

I have finished the job, I have told the whole story, described in detail the whole sequence of tragic events with which I was so strangely associated in the autumn of 1909. I have told the whole truth, omitted nothing, suppressed nothing – why should I? I have nothing to hide.

I found while writing that my memory had distinctly and vividly preserved a mass of detail – much of it quite trivial – scraps of conversation, ideas that passed through my mind, minor events of the day. In spite of this an entirely false idea developed in my mind about the length of time involved. I still have the impression that it was several weeks. But that is wrong. I still know the exact date on which Dr Gorski took me to the Bischoff villa to play in a quartet. It was 26 September 1909, a Sunday. In my mind's eye I can still see everything that happened on that day. In the post that morning there had been a letter from Norway, and I tried to make out the postmark, thinking of the girl student who had sat next to me at dinner during the trip across the Stavanger fjord. She had promised to write, but when I opened the envelope it only contained the prospectus of a winter-sports hotel on the Hardanger glacier. A disappointment.

Later I went to the fencing club. On the way, in the Florianigasse I was caught in a sudden heavy shower. I sheltered in a doorway, and discovered a stone baroque fountain in an old garden that had run wild. An old lady spoke to me and asked whether a charwoman named Kreutzer didn't live there. I still remember all that as if it were yesterday. Then the rain stopped and the fine weather returned. I remember

26 September 1909 as a day with warm wind and a cloudless sky.

I lunched in a garden restaurant with two officers of my regiment. I didn't read the morning papers till the afternoon. They contained articles on the Balkan question and the policy of the Young Turks – it's extraordinary how distinctly I remember all that. There was a leader on the King of England's tour, and another on the plans of the Sultan of Turkey. The first few lines were preceded by "Abdul Hamid's Waiting Game" in bold type. The "news of the day" sections gave details of the careers of Shefket Pasha and Niazi Bey – who remembers those names today? Overnight there had been a big fire at the Northwest station. "Huge stocks of timber destroyed", the headlines proclaimed. An academic society announced a performance of Büchner's *Danton*, the *Götterdämmerung* was on at the Opera, with a guest singer from Breslau as Hagen. Pictures by Jan Toorop and Lovis Corinth were being exhibited at the Kunstschau, and the whole town flocked there to gaze at them in amazement. Somewhere or other, in St Petersburg, I think, workers were rioting and striking, a church had been broken into at Salzburg, and there had been rowdy scenes in the Consulta in Rome. There was also a brief item in small type about the failure of the Bergstein bank. To me this came as no surprise, I had seen it coming and I withdrew my money in good time. But I couldn't help thinking about an acquaintance of mine, the actor Eugen Bischoff, who had also entrusted his funds to that bank. I should have warned him, I said to myself. But would he have believed me? He always regarded me as a retailer of false information. Why meddle in other people's affairs? I also remembered a conversation I had had a few days before with the director of the court theatre, in which Eugen Bischoff's name had cropped up. "He's getting old, unfortunately, I can't help him," the director had said, and had added some remarks about the pressure of the rising generation. If my impression was correct, there was little hope of Eugen Bischoff's contract being renewed, and now on top of that there was the disaster of the collapse of Bergstein and Co.

The twenty-sixth of September 1909 stands out so clearly in my mind that I still remember every detail distinctly. It all makes it the more inexplicable that I should have shifted to the middle of October the date on which the three of us went to the house in the Dominikanerbastei. Perhaps it was the memory of withered chestnut leaves on the garden paths, the ripe grapes being offered for sale at the street corners and the first autumn frosts, the whole complex of unconscious memories that are somehow associated with that day, that led me astray. That may well have been the case. In fact 30 September was the vital day. I established that with the aid of notes from the time that are still in my possession.

Thus the whole sinister and tragic business lasted five days only, from 26 to 30 September. The dramatic hunt for the culprit, the pursuit of an invisible enemy who was not of flesh and blood but a fearsome ghost from past centuries lasted for just five days. We found a trail of blood and followed it. A gateway to the past quietly opened. None of us suspected where it led, and it seems to me today that we groped painfully step by step down a long dark passage at the end of which a monster was waiting for us with upraised cudgel. The cudgel came down twice, three times, the last blow was meant for me, and I should have been done for and shared Eugen Bischoff's and Solgrub's dreadful fate had I not been snatched back to life in the nick of time.

How many victims may this bloodthirsty monster have found on his way through the thorn bushes of the centuries, in the course of his wanderings through different ages and different countries? I now look at many past destinies with different eyes. On the inside cover of the book I found a half-vanished signature among the names of previous owners. Have I deciphered it correctly? Could Heinrich von Kleist . . . ? No, there's no point in searching and guessing and invoking the names of the great and famous dead. They are shrouded in mist. The past remains silent, and no answer will ever come out of the darkness.

And it's not over yet, no, it's still there, visions still rise from the depths and force themselves upon me, at night and in broad daylight – though now, thank heaven, they are only pale and shadowy, insubstantial phantoms. The nerve in my brain has gone to sleep, but the sleep is still not deep enough. Sometimes sheer terror seizes me and sends me to the window, feeling that the dreadful waves of that terrible light must be rushing across the sky, and I cannot grasp the fact that overhead there's the sun, concealed in silvery mist or surrounded by purple clouds or alone in the endless blue and round me wherever I look are the old, familiar colours, those of the terrestrial world. Since that day I have never again seen that fearful trumpet red. But the shadows are there and keep coming back, they surround me, make as if to clutch me – will they never disappear from my life?

Perhaps. Perhaps the persecution is over. Perhaps I have got rid of the nightmare once and for all by writing it down. I have put my story, a pile of loose sheets of paper, behind me and said goodbye to it. What have I got to do with it now? I put it aside, as if someone else had been through all that or invented it, as if it had been written by someone else, not me.

There was also something else that prompted me to commit to paper everything that I wanted to forget and cannot.

Shortly before his death Solgrub destroyed a sheet of parchment that was covered with writing. He destroyed it to prevent anyone else from falling victim to that fearful error. But is it certain that that sheet of parchment was the only one of its kind? Is it not possible that in some forgotten corner of the world another copy of the Florentine organist's story may exist – yellowed with age, crumbling into dust, nibbled by rats, buried under piles of rubbish in a junk shop or hidden behind the tomes in an old library, or among the carpets, khanjars, and Koran covers on the floor of a bazaar in Erzingian, Diarbekir or

Jaipur – may it be lying in wait there, ready for resurrection and lusting after new prey?

We are all creatures who have disappointed the Creator's grand design. Without suspecting it we have a terrible enemy inside us. He lies there motionless, asleep, as if he were dead. Woe if he comes back to life. May no human being ever again set eyes on the trumpet red which I, God help me, have seen.

That is why I wrote my story. The pile of sheets of paper covered with writing that lies before me now does not have a proper beginning, I am very conscious of that.

How did it begin? I was sitting at my desk at home with my pipe between my teeth, smoking shag and leafing through a book, when Dr Gorski dropped in.

Dr Eduard Ritter von Gorski. During his lifetime he was hardly known outside the circle of his close colleagues, and only after his death did he become world famous. He died in Bosnia of an infectious disease on which he was a specialist.

I can still see him standing in front of me, slightly hunch-backed, badly shaved, carelessly dressed, his knitted tie all askew, holding his nose between his thumb and forefinger.

He began by scolding me. "That damned pipe of yours again," he exclaimed. "Can't you live without it? That abominable stink. You can smell it all the way down to the street."

"It's the smell of foreign railway stations, and I like it," I replied, and rose to greet him.

"The devil take it," he grumbled. "Where's your fiddle? You're coming to play at Eugen Bischoff's. I've been sent to fetch you."

I looked at him in surprise.

"Haven't you read the newspaper today?" I asked.

"So you know too?" he said. "Everyone seems to know except Eugen Bischoff himself. He hasn't an inkling. It's a bad business. I think everyone wants to keep it from him. Just when he's having difficulties with his director, and they don't want him to know anything until that's been settled. You really should have seen Dina today. She stands over him like a guardian angel. Come along, baron. She'll be glad of any kind of distraction today."

I had a burning desire to see Dina. But I was very careful. I acted as if I couldn't make up my mind, I must think it over.

"Just a little chamber music," Dr Gorski said to encourage me. "I have my cello downstairs in the cab. Perhaps a Brahms piano trio, if you'd like it."

To win me over he quietly whistled the first few bars of the scherzo in B major.

ONE

The room in which we played was on the raised ground floor of the villa, and the windows opened on to the garden. When I looked up from my music I could see the green doors of the pavilion in which Eugen Bischoff used to shut himself whenever he was sent a new part. That was where he studied and memorised it. Often he would be invisible for many hours, and late in the evening his silhouette would appear behind the lit windows, making strange gestures and movements that his role required of him.

The gravelled garden paths lay in dazzling sunshine. The deaf old villa gardener was crouching on the lawn between the beds of fuchsias and dahlias, cutting the grass with a never-changing movement of his right arm that made my eyes tired. Children were noisily playing with sailing-boats and flying kites in the next-door garden, and an old lady was sitting on a bench in the afternoon sun and feeding the sparrows with breadcrumbs from a bag. In the distance people taking a Sunday outing were pushing prams and carrying sunshades, strolling along a path through a meadow leading towards the woods.

We began at about four o'clock, and we had already played two Beethoven piano and violin sonatas and a Schubert trio. After tea it was at last time for the B major trio, which I love, particularly the first movement with its solemn rejoicing, and that was why I was annoyed when there was a knock at the door just after we had begun. Eugen Bischoff called out in that sonorous voice of his "Come in", and a young man came in. His face immediately struck me as familiar, though I couldn't remember where and in what circumstances I had seen it before. He shut the door by no means quietly, in spite of his obvious efforts not to disturb us. He was tall, very fair, broad-shouldered, and had an almost square head. I disliked him at first sight, and somehow he reminded me of a whale.

Dina looked up fleetingly from the piano when this belated guest came in. To my great pleasure she merely nodded casually to him and went on playing, while her husband rose noiselessly from the sofa to greet him. Over my music I saw the two whispering, and then the whale inquired, with an almost imperceptible interrogative movement of his head in my direction, who I was and what I was doing there. I concluded that he must feel very much at home here if he could permit himself such informality.

Eugen Bischoff introduced me to him as soon as we had finished.

"Engineer Waldemar Solgrub, a colleague of my brother-in-law – Baron von Yosch, who has been kind enough to stand in for Felix."

Felix, Dina's younger brother, heard himself being mentioned and waved his left hand, which was covered in a white bandage. He had burnt himself in his laboratory, and this prevented him from playing the violin. To make himself useful in spite of this he was turning the pages of the score.

Next came the turn of that friendly, smiling gnome Dr Gorski, but the engineer wasted practically no time at all shaking hands with him behind his cello, and a moment later he was talking to Dina Bischoff; and while he bent over her hand – which he held much longer than was necessary, which was actually painful to watch – while he stood there bending over her hand and talking to her urgently, I noticed that he was not quite so young as he had seemed at first. His closely cut fair hair was greying slightly at the temples and, though he behaved like a young man of twenty, he was probably getting on for forty.

At last he decided to release Dina's hand and he came over to me.

"I believe we have already met, have we not, Mr Virtuoso?" he said.

I answered very calmly and very politely.

"My name is Baron von Yosch."

The whale swallowed the rebuke and apologised. As so often happens, he said, he had not heard my name correctly when we were introduced. He had a way of spouting out the words when he spoke that reminded me of a whale spouting out its jet of water.

"But you do remember me, don't you?" he said.

"No, I'm very sorry, I don't."

"Five weeks ago, if I'm not mistaken . . ."

"I'm afraid you are mistaken. Five weeks ago I was travelling abroad."

"Quite right, in Norway, and we sat facing each other for four hours between Christiania and Bergen. Isn't that so?"

He stirred the teacup that Dina put in front of him. She overheard what he had just said and looked at us curiously.

"So you two have met before?" she said.

The whale chuckled quietly and said, turning to Dina:

"Yes, but on the trip across the Hardanger fjeld Baron von Yosch was just as uncommunicative as he is today."

"That's very likely, that's the way I am, I'm afraid, I seldom make friends with strangers when I'm travelling abroad," I replied, and so far as I was concerned that was the end of the matter.

But it wasn't the end of the matter for the whale. Eugen Bischoff, who was always prepared to attribute all sorts of talents and outstanding characteristics to his friends, made a remark of some sort about the amazing memory for faces that the engineer had once more demonstrated.

"Oh, there was really nothing very remarkable about it on this occasion," he said, sipping his tea. "You'll forgive me, baron, won't you, but your face really does not stand out from hundreds of others, your resemblance to many other people is really very striking. But that English pipe of yours is an

3

entirely different matter, its distinctive characteristics enabled me to recognise you at once."

I found his joking rather crude, and thought he was paying me rather too much attention. I really did not know what entitled me to that honour.

"But now, Eugen, old boy, it's time you told us all about it," he said in loud and self-assured tones. "I see you were a great success in Berlin, the newspapers were full of it. And how are you getting on with your Richard III? Well, I hope?"

"Shall we go on playing?" I suggested.

The whale made an exaggeratedly alarmed and defensive gesture of apology.

"You haven't finished yet?" he exclaimed. "I beg pardon a thousand times. Really, I thought . . . alas, I'm completely unmusical."

I assured him with the greatest courtesy and friendliness that this had not escaped me.

He ignored this remark, sat down, stretched his legs, picked up some photographs from the table, and became immersed in contemplation of one of them, showing Eugen Bischoff in the role of some Shakespearean king.

I began tuning my fiddle.

"We just took a short interval between the first and second movements – in honour of your arrival, Herr Solgrub," said Dr Gorski, and behind me I heard Dina whispering:

"Why are you so unfriendly to him?" she said.

At that I flushed scarlet, as I always did when she spoke to me. I turned my head, and saw the strange oval of her face and her dark eyes looking at me questioningly and in surprise, and I sought for an answer, wanted to explain to her that I was prejudiced against people who came crashing into rooms at such inopportune moments. True, they didn't do it on purpose, they couldn't help it, they might be the best people in the world, I was being unfair to them, as I was very well aware. But an unhappy constitutional defect made them always turn up at the wrong moment. I gladly admitted that – but I

4

couldn't suppress my antipathy, I just couldn't, it was impossible, it was my nature . . .

No, it was all lies. Whom was I trying to deceive? It was
jealousy, just pitiful jealousy, the pain of disappointed love.
When I saw Dina I became her watch-dog keeping guard over
her. Anyone who approached her was my deadly enemy. I
wanted to keep for myself alone every word that she spoke,
every glance of her eyes. Why couldn't I escape from her, get
up and go and put an end to it once and for all? It ached and
burned inside me.

But hush. Dr Gorski tapped his music stand twice with his
bow, and we began the second movement.

TWO

How often have the rhythms of that second movement filled me with fear and trembling. I have never been able to play it right through without succumbing to deep melancholy, though my passionate love is associated with it.

Yes, it's a scherzo, but what a scherzo. It begins with a dreadful merriment, a gaiety that makes one's blood run cold. Eerie laughter sweeps through the room, a wild and grim carnival of cloven-hoofed forms. That is how this strange scherzo begins; and suddenly from the midst of this infernal Bacchanal there arises a solitary human voice, the voice of a lost soul, a soul in a torment of fear that soars upwards and laments its suffering.

But the satanic laughter breaks out again, smashes loudly into the pure harmonies and tears the song to shreds. Once more the voice arises, softly and hesitantly, and finds its melody and bears it aloft as if wanting to escape with it to another world. But the devils of hell are triumphant, the day has come, the last day, the Day of Judgment. Satan triumphs over the sinful soul and the lamenting human voice falls from the heights and disappears in a Judas-like laughter of despair.

When the movement ended no-one spoke. The silence round me lasted for several minutes.

Then the gloomy, disconsolate world of shadows in which I was plunged suddenly vanished. The dream of the crack of doom, the nightmare of the Day of Judgment faded and left me free.

6

Dr Gorski had risen to his feet and was pacing slowly up and down, Eugen Bischoff was in a brown study, and the engineer had a good stretch as if he had just woken up. Then he helped himself to a cigarette from the box on the table and snapped the lid shut.

My eyes turned to Dina Bischoff. One's first thought when one wakes up in the morning is often the last one had when falling asleep the night before, and all I could think of now that the movement was finished was how angry she had been with me and how vital it was for me to make it up with her, and the longer I looked at her the stronger became the need to do so. I could think of nothing else, and presumably this childish need was an after-effect of the music.

She turned her head to me.

"Well, baron, why are you so deep in thought?" she said. "What are you thinking about?"

"I was thinking about my dog Zamor," I replied.

I knew very well why I said that, I looked her straight in the eye as I did so, both of us knew very well indeed. She knew that dog, oh, how well she knew it.

She winced, pretended not to hear, and turned away angrily. Now I had really upset her. I should not have said that, I should not have reminded her of my small dog Zamor just at the moment when that stranger, that whale, was certainly uppermost in her thoughts.

Meanwhile Dr Gorski had put his cello and bow back into its linen case.

"I think that will be enough for today," he said. "We'll spare Herr Solgrub the third movement, shan't we?"

Dina threw her head back and hummed the theme of the adagio.

"Listen," she said, "it makes you feel you're sitting in a boat, doesn't it?"

To my surprise the whale also started humming the theme of the third movement. He actually did so almost faultlessly, only a trifle too fast. Then he said:

"Sitting in a boat? No. I think it's the gliding rhythm that

7

leads you astray. At all events it puts quite different ideas into my head."

"I see you know the B major trio very well," I said. This remark seemed to make things up between me and Dina. She immediately started talking to me.

"I must explain to you that our friend Solgrub is by no means as unmusical as he makes out," she said eagerly. "It's just that he feels obliged to display a superiority to music and all the other useless arts. Isn't that true, Waldemar, it's what your profession demands of you, isn't it? And he tries to persuade me that he accepts my husband as an actor only because he has seen his photo on picture postcards and in an illustrated weekly. Keep quiet, Waldemar, I know all about you."

The whale acted as if all this had nothing to do with him. He took a book from the shelf and started looking through it. But he obviously liked being talked about and being explained and analysed by Dina.

Her brother now intervened.

"And at the same time he's more deeply affected by music than any of us," he said. "It's the Russian soul, don't you see. He immediately sees whole pictures in his mind: a landscape, or the sea with clouds and breakers, or a sunset, or the movements of a human being, or – what was it just now? – a flock of fleeing cassowaries, I think, and heaven knows what else besides."

"The other day," Dina went on, "when I played him the last movement of the Appassionata – it was the Appassionata, wasn't it, Waldemar, that put the strange idea of a swearing and cursing old soldier into your head?"

So the two of them have got as far as that already, I said to myself, full of bitterness and rage. She plays Beethoven sonatas for him. That's exactly how things had begun between Dina and me once upon a time.

The whale put down his book.

"The Appassionata, third movement," he said thoughtfully, and leaned back and shut his eyes. "It makes me see – with a clarity that it's impossible to describe at this moment – but at the time I could describe every button on his uniform – I see a cripple with a wooden leg, an aged, disabled veteran of Napoleon's campaigns, raging and cursing as he limps round the room."

"Raging and cursing? Poor devil. But he had probably managed to lay aside a little money for a rainy day."

I said that quite unintentionally and without thinking, I meant it merely as a joke, and only a moment later did I realise what a painful effect that remark was bound to have; and indeed, Dr Gorski shook his head disapprovingly, Felix looked at me angrily and put his bandaged hand admonishingly to his mouth, and Dina looked at me in shocked amazement. There was a moment of dismayed silence, and I felt myself flushing with embarrassment. But Eugen Bischoff had noticed nothing. He turned to the engineer and said:

"I've often envied your ability to visualise things so vividly," and at that moment the idol of the gallery, the hero of the drama schools, looked very depressed. "You ought to have been an actor, my dear Solgrub."

"What a thing to say, Bischoff!" Dr Gorski exclaimed almost violently. "You, who are chock-full of characters and personalities. They're piled up on top of one another inside you, kings and rebels, chancellors and popes, murderers, rogues and archangels, beggars and God knows who else besides."

"But never in my life have I visualised a single one of them as vividly as Solgrub visualised his wooden-legged old soldier. All I've seen is their shadows, I've never seen anything but vague, shapeless, colourless, unsubstantial forms having a faint resemblance now to one character, now to another. If I had been able to visualise the button on that uniform, like Solgrub, good God, what an impersonator of human character I should have been."

I understand the resignation implicit in his words. He was an old man, no longer the great Eugen Bischoff. People let him feel this, and he felt it himself, though he fought the feeling and refused to admit it to himself. Oh, the sad hopelessness of the years to come, the years of your decline, my unhappy friend.

Suddenly the conversation with the director flashed through my mind, and I remembered what he had told me. Suppose someone passed on the information, suppose I myself . . . You know, dear Eugen, I'm on excellent terms with your director, we discuss all sorts of things, and recently – I can tell you, Eugen, you won't take it tragically – a few days ago he told me, only jestingly, of course . . .

Good God, what an idea. Heaven forbid that he should find out, it would be the end of him. Emotionally he's so vulnerable, so devoid of any inner prop, a puff of wind would be enough to bowl him over.

Dina's brother was now talking to him. That excellent young man was resorting to all the stage jargon that he knew: the importance of psychological detail and of entering into the spirit of the play, and so on and so forth – but Eugen Bischoff shook his head.

"Don't build castles in the air for me, Felix," he said. "You know as well as I do what I lack. What you say is quite right, but it doesn't go to the heart of the matter. Take it from me, those things can be learnt, or can come by themselves with the task one is facing. But creative imagination cannot be learnt. You have it or you don't. I lack the imagination that can create a world out of nothing, and many others, in fact most, lack it too. Yes, Dina, I know what you are going to say. I've made my way in the world, there are some things I can do, never mind what the papers say. But do any of you suspect what a dry, prosaic person I really am? Something happens that ought to give one sleepless nights, send cold shudders down one's spine and give one nightmares, but heaven knows that the effect on me is not very different from reading reports of accidents in the paper at breakfast in the morning."

"Have you seen today's paper?" I interrupted. I was thinking of the workers' riots in St Petersburg. Eugen Bischoff was very interested in social questions.

"No," he replied. "I looked for it everywhere, but couldn't find it. Dina, what happened to the paper this morning?"

Dina went white and red and white again. Good heavens, I should have remembered that they had kept from him the newspaper with the news of the failure of his bank. I had put my foot in it again. I was committing one *faux pas* after another.

But Dina recovered her composure quickly.

"The paper?" she said casually, in tones as matter-of-fact as if she were mentioning something of no importance whatever. "I think I saw it somewhere in the garden. I'll find it again. But Eugen, please go on, you were telling us something so interesting."

Dina's brother was standing next to me.

"Do you propose to go on with your experiments?" he hissed softly into my ear without moving his lips.

What did he mean by that? What was he trying to say?

I had thoughtlessly committed a *faux pas*, and that was all. What else could it have been?

THREE

Eugen Bischoff paced up and down, he had something on his mind, he seemed to be trying to put something into words. Then he stopped right in front of me and looked at me. He looked me in the face, scrutinising me with a troubled, uncertain, almost mistrustful expression. The way he did so made me feel uncomfortable, I don't really know why.

"It's a strange business, baron," he said. "It may make you feel hot and cold when I tell you about it. Perhaps it will keep you awake all night, that's the sort of thing it is. Up here" – and he vigorously tapped his brow – "there's a nerve inside me that dislikes being disturbed and won't co-operate properly. It's there only for minor matters, the petty, everyday things of life. But for fear and horror and anger and raging anxiety it's useless. I lack the organ to deal with them."

"Then tell us about it, Bischoff," Dr Gorski interrupted.

"I don't really know whether I'll be able to make you understand what an extraordinary story it is. Telling a story has never been my forte. Perhaps the whole thing won't strike you as being so disturbing. As I was saying . . ."

"Why all this beating about the bush, Eugen?" said the engineer, tapping his cigarette over the ashtray.

"Very well, then, listen, this is the story, make of it what you will. Some time ago I met a young naval officer who had been given several months' compassionate leave to settle his family affairs. These were of a peculiar kind.

"He had had a younger brother here in Vienna who was a painter and a student at the Academy. He seems to have been very talented – I've seen some of his work, a group of children, a nurse and a girl bathing. Well, one day this young man committed suicide. It was completely unmotivated, there was nothing whatever to explain such an act of total despair. He had no debts or other money troubles, no love trouble and no illness – in short, the suicide could not have been more mysterious. And his brother . . ."

"Such cases are more frequent than one thinks," Dr Gorski interrupted. "They are generally disposed of in the police reports by resorting to the phrase 'while the balance of his mind was temporarily disturbed'."

"Yes, that was what happened in this case, but the family were not satisfied. The parents in particular thought it inconceivable that their son should have killed himself without leaving behind a letter for them. Not even the one-line note usual in these cases – 'Dear mama, papa, forgive me, I could not do otherwise' – was found among his papers, and earlier letters gave no hint of any suicidal tendencies. So the family refused to believe it was suicide, and the elder brother came to Vienna determined to do everything possible to throw light on the matter.

"He had a fixed plan which he carried out doggedly. He lived in his brother's flat, assumed his daily habits and daily routine, and sought out and made the acquaintance of everyone with whom his brother associated or came into contact, and he avoided opportunities of meeting anyone else. He became a pupil at the Academy, he drew and he painted and spent a few hours every day at the café where his brother had been a regular customer, and he even went so far as to wear his dead brother's clothes and join an elementary Italian class that his brother had attended; and he never missed a lesson, though as a naval officer his command of Italian was complete. He did all this in the belief that in this way he was bound eventually to stumble on the cause of his brother's puzzling death, and nothing would divert him from his purpose.

"He led this life, which was not really his but someone else's, for two whole months, and I can't say whether it brought him any nearer his objective. But one day he came back to his lodgings very late. His landlady, who took up his dinner, noticed this because it was in striking contrast to his usual habits, which were marked by meticulous punctuality. He was not actually in a bad mood, though he made some irritable remarks about the food, which had got cold. He told the landlady he wanted to go to the opera that evening and hoped he would still be able to get tickets, and ordered a cold supper in his room for eleven o'clock.

"A quarter of an hour later the cook took up his black coffee. The door was locked, but she could hear the young officer striding up and down the room. She knocked at the door and called out: 'Your coffee, sir,' and left the cup on a chair outside the door. Some time later she went up again to fetch the empty cup, but it was still outside the door and had not been touched. She knocked, but there was no answer, she listened, but nothing stirred, and suddenly she heard voices and brief cries in a language she did not understand, and soon afterwards there was a loud cry.

"She shook the door, called out, raised the alarm, the landlady arrived, the two of them forced the door – and the room was empty. But the windows were open, there was a noise down in the street, and they realised what had happened. Down below a crowd had gathered round a body. Half a minute before, the young officer had flung himself from the window – his cigarette was still glowing on the desk."

The engineer interrupted the story.

"Flung himself from the window?" he exclaimed. "That's amazing. As an officer he must have had a weapon in his possession."

"Quite right. His revolver was found in a drawer of his desk. It was unloaded and intact. An army 9mm. revolver. The ammunition was in the same drawer, a whole boxful."

"Go on, go on," Dr Gorski urged the actor.

"Go on? But that's the whole story. He had committed suicide, like his brother before him. I don't know whether he had found the answer to his riddle. But, if he had, he must have had his reasons for taking the secret with him."

"What are you saying?" Dr Gorski exclaimed. "Surely he left behind a letter or note, at any rate a line or two of explanation to his parents?"

"No."

This emphatic reply came, not from Eugen Bischoff, but from the engineer, who went on:

"He had no time, don't you see? That's the extraordinary thing about the case, he had no time. He had no time to fetch his revolver and load it. How could he have had time to write a letter?"

"You're wrong, Solgrub," Eugen Bischoff said. "He did leave writing behind. True, it was only part of a single word . . ."

"I call that military brevity," said Dr Gorski; and an amused twinkle in his eyes indicated to me that he regarded the whole story as fiction.

"Also," said Eugen Bischoff, finishing his story, "the tip of his pencil broke and the paper was torn at that point."

"And the word? What was it?"

"It was hastily scribbled and almost illegible. It was 'dreadful'."

No-one spoke. Only the engineer let out a brief and sharp "Oh!" of surprise. Dina had risen and switched on the lamp. Now it was light in the room, but the feeling of oppression to which I, like all the others, had succumbed would not go away.

Only Dr Gorski was sceptical.

"Admit it, Bischoff," he said. "You made up the whole story to make our flesh creep, didn't you?"

Eugen Bischoff shook his head.

"No, doctor, I didn't make up anything. It all happened less than a week ago just as I described it. The most extraordinary things happen, you can take it from me, doctor. What do you think about it, Solgrub?"

"It was murder," the engineer replied briefly and firmly. "A very unusual kind of murder, but murder, that's obvious to me. But who was the murderer? How did he get into the room and where did he vanish to? One will have to think about it very carefully when one's on one's own."

He looked at his watch.

"It's late, and I must go."

"Nonsense, you're all staying for supper," Eugen Bischoff announced, "and afterwards we'll all stay for a while and talk about more cheerful things."

"How would it be, for instance, if the distinguished audience of connoisseurs assembled here were privileged to hear extracts from your new role?" Dr Gorski said.

In a few days' time Eugen Bischoff was to play Richard III for the first time; that had been in all the newspapers, but he did not welcome Dr Gorski's suggestion. He twisted his mouth and frowned.

"Not today," he said. "Another time I'll do it with pleasure."

Dina and her brother set vigorously about trying to persuade him to change his mind. Why not today? Why be so temperamental? When everyone would enjoy it so much.

"Those enjoying the privilege of knowing you personally, Bischoff," Dr Gorski announced, "are surely entitled to some precedence over the common herd in the boxes and the stalls."

Eugen Bischoff shook his head and refused to give in.

"No, not today, it just wouldn't do. You'd hear something that's simply not ready for performance yet, and I don't want that."

"A kind of dress rehearsal before close friends," the engineer suggested.

"No, you mustn't press me. Normally I don't refuse, in fact I enjoy doing what you ask, but today it's out of the question. I haven't visualised Richard yet, I must be able to see him standing in front of me, it's essential."

Dr Gorski apparently gave in, but he once more slyly twinkled at me, for he had an excellent and well tried method of overcoming the actor's resistance, and had decided to use it now. He set about it very cautiously and cleverly by talking with the most innocent expression on his face about a very mediocre Berlin actor whom he said he had seen playing the part. He praised the man's performance highly.

"You know I'm not a mere gallery fan, Bischoff, but that Semblinsky – he's simply marvellous," he said. "The ideas the man has. The way he sits on the palace steps, throws his glove up in the air and catches it, and then lies down and stretches out like a cat in the sunshine. And then there's the way he builds up the soliloquy."

And to give Eugen Bischoff an idea of what the man's performance was like he began declaiming with passionate gestures and much pathos:

"Cheated of feature by dissembling nature
Unfinished, deformed . . ."

He interrupted himself with some textual criticism. "No, it's the other way round, deformed comes first. Never mind.

"Deformed, unfinished, sent before my time
Into this breathing world – "

At this point the actor interrupted, still very gently. "That's enough, doctor," he said.

"Into this breathing world – don't interrupt me, please –
scarce half made up
And that so lamely and unfashionable
That dogs bark at me as I halt by them . . ."

"That's enough," Bischoff exclaimed, putting his hands to his ears. "Stop! You make me feel ill."

But Dr Gorski was not to be put off so easily.

"Why I, in this piping time of peace
Have no delight to pass away the time;
Unless to spy my shadow in the sun,
And descant on mine own deformity.
And therefore – since I cannot prove a lover

To entertain these fair well-spoken days –
I am determined to prove a villain . . ."

"And I'm determined to wring your neck if you don't stop,"
Eugen Bischoff declared threateningly. "I ask you, you turn
Gloucester into a sentimental clown. Richard III is a beast of
prey, a monster, a brute – but yet he's a man and a king, not
a hysterical buffoon, damn it."

He began pacing excitedly up and down the room, carried
away by the part. Then he suddenly stopped. What happened
next was exactly what Dr Gorski had expected.

"I'll show you how to play Richard III. But quiet, please,
I'll give you the soliloquy."

"I have my own conception of the character," Dr Gorski
said with cool impertinence. "But please – you're the actor,
I'm always willing to learn."

Eugen Bischoff rewarded him with a glance full of malice
and contempt. In the process of transforming himself into the
Shakespearean king he was no longer faced with Dr Gorski,
but with his wretched brother Clarence.

"Listen," he said. He rapped out the word as if he were
giving an order. "I'm going over to the pavilion for a few
minutes. Meanwhile open the window. It's intolerable here
because of the smoke. I shan't be long."

"Are you going to put on make-up? Why, Eugen? We'll do
without it," Dina's brother said.

Eugen Bischoff's eyes flickered and shone. Never before
had I seen him in such a state of excitation, and he said something very strange.

"Make-up? No. What I want is to see the button on the
uniform. You must leave me alone for a while. I'll be back in
a couple of minutes."

He went out, but came back immediately.

"Listen," he said. "That Semblinsky, that great Semblinsky
of yours. Do you know what he is? He's a fool. I once saw
him as Iago, it was a disaster."

Then he went. I saw him walking quickly across the garden,

18

talking to himself and gesticulating, he was already in the world of Richard III, in Baynard's Castle. In his hurry he nearly knocked over his old gardener, who was still kneeling on the lawn cutting the grass, though by now it was quite dark outside. Then he disappeared, and a moment later the pavilion windows were brightly lit, scattering tremulous shafts of light and shifting shadows into the big, quiet, night-time garden.

FOUR

Dr Gorski was still declaiming Shakespearean verse with false pathos and absurdly extravagant gestures. Eugen Bischoff having left the room, he did this partly out of sheer enthusiasm for Shakespeare, partly out of pig-headedness, and partly to pass the time pending the actor's return. Being completely carried away by this time, he had got to *King Lear* and, to the distress of the rest of us, insisted on singing the jester's songs in that hoarse voice of his to any tune that came into his head. Meanwhile the engineer sat silently in his armchair, chain-smoking and gazing at the pattern of the carpet at his feet. He could not get the young naval officer's story out of his head, his tragic and puzzling suicide left him no peace. Every now and then he started up and looked with amazement at the singing doctor, shaking his head as at a strange and extraordinary phenomenon, and once he tried to drag him back to the world of rational reality.

He leaned forward and took Dr Gorski's wrist.

"Listen, doctor, there's one thing that I simply can't understand. Listen to me for a moment, please. Let us assume it was suicide on a sudden impulse. But in that case why did he lock himself in his room a quarter of an hour beforehand? Why should he lock himself in his room if he was thinking of suicide? Why? Explain that to me, please."

> "That lord that counsell'd thee
> To give away thy land
> Come place him here by me
> Do thou for him stand . . ."

20

That was Dr Gorski's only reply, apart from an irritable gesture as if he were shooing away a fly that was bothering him. "Oh, stop that nonsense," the engineer said to him. "He locked the door a quarter of an hour beforehand. So the presumption is that he had plenty of time to make his preparations. But then he jumped out of the window. An officer who has a revolver and a whole box of ammunition in a drawer of his desk does not do that."

Dr Gorski did not allow himself to be diverted by such considerations from his Shakespearean recitation. The small, slightly malformed gnome, standing in the middle of the room, completely carried away by his performance and plucking the strings of an imaginary lute, provided a comic interlude when he sang

"The sweet and bitter fool
Will presently appear . . ."

The engineer at last realised the hopelessness of trying to get him to take an interest in his theories, and he turned to me.

"The two things are mutually exclusive, don't you agree?" he said. "Don't let me forget to ask Eugen Bischoff about it before we go."

"Where has my sister vanished to?" Felix suddenly asked.

"She was quite right to leave, there's much too much smoke in the room," Solgrub said, stubbing out his cigarette. "*Magna pars fui*, it's largely my fault, I admit. We should have opened the window, but forgot."

No-one noticed when I got up and left the room, noiselessly shutting the door behind me. I hoped I would find Dina in the garden. I walked round the path that surrounded the lawn until I reached the wooden fence of the next-door garden, but she was not in any of her usual places. There was an open book on the garden table under the slope, and the leaves felt damp from the rain of the past few days or from the evening dew. Once I thought I could see someone in a recess in the wall and thought it must be Dina, but when I drew near it turned out to be some gardening tools, two empty watering cans, a basket, a rake propped up against the wall and a torn hammock moving in the wind.

I don't know how long I stayed in the garden. It may have been a long time. I may have been leaning against a tree and dreaming.

Suddenly I heard the sound of voices and loud laughter from the room, and someone's hand swept high-spiritedly up the keys of the piano from the lowest octaves to the shrill highest notes. Felix's figure appeared like a big, dark shadow at the open window.

"Hi, is that you, Eugen?" he called down into the garden. "No, it isn't, it's you, baron. Where have you been all this time?"

There was suddenly an anxious note in his voice.

Dr Gorski appeared behind him, he recognised me, and began declaiming.

"Here, in the moon's pale light, we meet . . ."

He broke off, because one of the two others dragged him away from the window, and I heard him call out: "How dare you, traitor?"

Then all was quiet again. Light suddenly appeared on the first floor over their heads. Dina appeared on the veranda and started laying the table for supper in the milky glow of the standard lamp.

I went back towards the house and up the wooden steps to the veranda. Dina heard my footsteps, turned and shaded her eyes with her hand.

"Is that you, Gottfried?" she said.

I sat silently facing her and watched as she arranged the plates and glasses on the white tablecloth. I listened to her deep and steady breathing, she breathed like a dreamlessly sleeping child. The wind bent and shook the branches of the chestnut trees and swept small cavalcades of withered autumn leaves before it down the gravel path. Down in the garden the old gardener was still at work. He had lit his lantern, which was next to him on the lawn, and its melancholy glow mingled with the broad band of steady bright light coming from the windows of the pavilion.

Suddenly I started.

Someone had called out my name – "Yosch!" – just my name, nothing else, but in the sound of that voice there was something that startled me – anger, reproach, horror and surprise . . .

Dina stopped laying the table and listened. Then she looked at me inquiringly and with surprise in her voice.

"That was Eugen," she said. "What can he be wanting?"

Then Eugen cried out a second time. "Dina! Dina!" he cried, but his voice was completely changed, there was no more anger or surprise in it, but anguish, grief and infinite despair.

"I'm here, Eugen, I'm here," she cried, leaning out over the garden.

For two or three seconds there was no reply. Then a shot rang out, followed immediately by another.

I saw Dina start back, she stood there unable to speak or move. I couldn't stay with her, I had to go down and find out what had happened. I think I remember that at the first moment I had a distinct impression of two intruders who had climbed over the garden fence to steal fruit. I don't know how it happened, but I found myself in a dark, unfamiliar room on the raised ground floor. I couldn't find the way out, and I couldn't find the window or the electric-light switch. There was nothing but the wall everywhere, and I struck my brow painfully against something with a sharp edge. I groped about in the dark for some minutes getting angrier and angrier and more and more dismayed.

Then I heard footsteps, a door opened, a match flared up in the darkness, and I found myself face to face with the engineer.

"What was it? What happened?" I asked, full of alarm and fear, yet glad that there was light at last and that I was no longer alone. "What was it? What happened?" The idea of thieves breaking in that had formed in my mind hardened into a distinct vision I was convinced I had actually seen. I was now sure I had seen three of them. One of them, a short, bearded man, was clinging to the top of the fence, another was just rising from the ground while the third, using the bushes and tree-trunks as cover, ran towards the pavilion with long, loping strides.

"What happened?" I asked yet again. The match went out, and the engineer's pale and distraught face disappeared in the darkness.

"I'm looking for Dina," I heard him say. "We mustn't let her go to him. It's terrible. One of us must stay with her."

"She's up on the veranda."

"How could you leave her alone?" he exclaimed, and a moment later he was outside.

I found the music room. It was empty, and outside the door a chair had been upset.

I went down to the garden. I still remember the torment of impatience I felt for a brief moment because the garden path was so long and seemed never-ending.

The pavilion door was open, and I went in.

I knew at once, even before I looked into the room. I knew what had happened. I knew that there had been no struggle with intruders, but that Eugen Bischoff had committed suicide. Where my certainty came from I cannot say.

He lay next to the desk with his face turned in my direction. His coat and waistcoat were unbuttoned, and he had a revolver in his stiffly outstretched right hand. In falling he had brought down two books, the inkstand and a small marble bust of Iffland. Dr Gorski was kneeling on the floor beside him.

He was still alive when I got there. He opened his eyes, his hand trembled, his head moved. Or was that an illusion? His face was slightly distorted with pain, and when he recognised me, or so I thought, it assumed an expression of indescribable, overwhelming surprise.

He tried to sit up, he wanted to speak, groaned, and fell back. Dr Gorski held his left hand. But that puzzling expression of infinite surprise lasted for only a brief moment. Then it turned into a grimace of blazing hatred.

Those hate-filled eyes were directed at me, and so they remained and would not let me go. They were directed at me, at me alone, and I did not, could not understand what he was trying to say to me. Also I could not understand, it was utterly unintelligible to me that I, faced with a dying man, felt no awe or terror or shock, but merely a slight discomfort at the way he looked at me and a dread of coming into contact with the bloodstain on the carpet, which was getting bigger and bigger all the time.

Dr Gorski rose to his feet. Eugen Bischoff's face, normally so mobile, had turned into a stiff, pale, silent mask.

I heard Felix call out from the door:

"She's coming, she's in the garden, doctor, what are we to do?"

Dr Gorski had taken a mackintosh from the wall and spread it over Eugen Bischoff's lifeless body.

"Go and meet her, doctor," Felix implored. "Talk to her, I can't."

I saw Dina approaching the pavilion, and the engineer was with her, trying to stop her. I was suddenly overcome with an immense weariness, I found standing difficult, I wanted to fling myself down on the lawn to rest. It's nothing, I said to myself, just a passing weakness, perhaps because of the way I rushed through the garden just now.

And, while Dina disappeared through the door of the pavilion I had a strange experience.

It was the deaf gardener. He was standing beside me, bending over the grass, still working away as if nothing had happened.

So far as he was concerned, nothing had happened. To him everything was as it had been before. He had not heard the cry or the shots. But now he must have felt my eyes on him, for he stood up and looked at me.

"You called me, sir," he said.

I shook my head. No, I hadn't called him.

He didn't believe me. The muffled, confused noise that reached his deaf ears had given him a vague idea that someone had called his name.

"But you did call me, sir," he said grumpily, but he was still suspicious of me and kept me under observation, looking at me sideways while he went on with his work.

And only now was I overcome with the horror I had not felt when faced with Eugen Bischoff's body, but now it was suddenly there, and shock sent ice-cold shivers down my spine.

No, I had not called him. But the way he stood there and stared at me and swung the sickle as he cut the grass: he was the deaf elderly gardener, but for a moment he looked like the figure of death in an old picture.

FIVE

It lasted only for a moment, and then I regained control of my nerves and my senses. I shook my head, I could not help smiling at the fact that in a waking dream I had seen in that simple old servant of the household the silent messenger, the ferryman across the everlasting stream. Slowly I walked down the garden until I reached the edge of the slope, and there, at a concealed spot between the fence and the greenhouse I found a table and a bench, and sat down.

It must have rained, or was it the evening dew? The wet leaves and branches of the elderberry bushes brushed against my face, a drop of water trickled down my hand. There must have been some spruce or pine trees not far away, I could not see them in the dark, but their smell reached me.

It did me good to sit there. I breathed in the cool, damp garden air, I let the wind stroke my face, and I listened to the breathing of the night. Inside me there was a quietly nagging anxiety, I was afraid they might have missed me and be looking for me, and that they might find me here. No, I must remain alone, there was no-one to whom I could talk at that moment. I was afraid of meeting Dina and her brother – what, at that moment, could I have said to them? Nothing but empty words of pitifully inadequate commiseration, the triviality of which filled me with horror.

It was clear to me that my disappearance would be taken for what at the deepest level it really was – flight from the gravity of the hour. But I didn't mind. I remembered that I had often done the same thing as a child. On my mother's name day, when I should have recited the carefully inculcated verses and good wishes, I had been afflicted by similar fears, and took refuge somewhere where no-one could find me, and reappeared only when everything was over.

The sound of a mouth organ floated over to me from the open kitchen window of a neighbouring house. A few bars of a stupid, vacuous waltz I had heard a thousand times before, the *Valse bleue* or *Souvenir de Moscou*, I couldn't remember what it was called. How did it come about that it had such a deeply calming effect on me, that all the weight that had been crushing me suddenly lifted? The *Valse bleue*, an appropriate dirge for the death of a human being. Over on the pavilion floor lay someone who was no longer a fellow human being but belonged to another world, had become incomprehensible and strange. But where was the shudder of awe, the shudder of the tragic, the inconceivable and the unalterable? The *Valse bleue*. The rhythm of life and death was a banal dance tune. Thus we come and thus we go. What shatters us and casts us down utterly turns out to be an ironic smile on the face of the world spirit, to whom suffering and grief and death are continually recurring phenomena familiar since the beginning of time.

The music suddenly stopped, and for several minutes there was deep silence, with nothing but raindrops dripping from the branches of the maple trees and the glass roof of the greenhouse. Then the mouth organ started up again, this time with a march. Somewhere not far away a church clock struck. I counted the strokes. It was ten o'clock. Was it as late as that? And here I was sitting and listening to a mouth organ, while over there Dina and her brother . . . perhaps they needed me, they were bound to be looking for me, Dina couldn't possibly think of everything herself.

It struck me that there were a large number of things that had to be attended to. In a case like this the police must be sent for and the authorities informed, the medical officer of health must be sent for, and the undertaker – and here I was sitting and listening to music from a kitchen window. And of course the press must be told. Of course Dina could not possibly think of everything herself. What were her friends for? Nothing about suicide must be allowed to get into the papers. Someone must hire a cab and make the round of the newspaper offices. Sudden death of a great actor, a beloved artist. At the height of his powers. Irreplaceable loss to the German stage. The many thousands of his admirers. The grief-stricken family.

And then there was the theatre management: no-one had given them a thought. It was essential that next week's playbill be altered, and there was no time to lose. It was Sunday, would anybody still be on duty at the office at this time of night? It was ten o'clock, someone must telephone immediately or – better still – I must get in touch with the director. To think that I, a friend of the family, had not thought of that before.

I wanted to get up and go immediately. I was seized with an irresistible impulse to act, to do whatever was necessary, to take full responsibility for all the needs of the hour. We must telephone at once, I said to myself again, in five minutes it may be too late – nobody will be left in the office – Richard III on Tuesday – but in spite of all this I just went on sitting there limply and feebly and dead tired, incapable of carrying out any of my intentions.

I'm ill, I murmured to myself and made another attempt to get up. Oh, of course, I'm feverish, sitting in the cold night air without hat or coat, and getting wet into the bargain. It may be the death of me. I took the newspaper from my pocket, heaven knows why I had brought it with me, I carefully spread it out on the bench so that I shouldn't have to sit in the damp, and suddenly I heard my old doctor's voice, I heard it as distinctly as if he were standing beside me.

"Oh dear, baron, so we're unwell, are we? Been overdoing things a bit lately, haven't we, and feeling rather tired? Well, what about a few days in bed, two or three perhaps, we have plenty of time at our disposal, haven't we, and we shan't be missing anything. We'll keep well covered up, shan't we, and hot tea certainly won't do us any harm, and no letters, no newspapers and no visitors will do us good, yes, a great deal of good, won't it? So let us take the good old doctor's advice and go straight home, there's nothing for us to do here, we're really ill, feverish, aren't we? Just let me feel your pulse . . ."

I obediently held out my hand and awoke from dream and sleep and there I was, sitting alone on the cold, wet bench. I really felt ill, I was shivering with cold, my teeth were chattering wildly. I wanted to go home, I wanted to slip away without saying goodbye, I wasn't wanted here, there was no-one here who needed me. Dina and Felix knew what to do, and besides, Dr Gorski was there, I was in everyone's way.

Good night, garden, and good night to you too, mouth organ, my companion during this lonely hour – and good night to you for ever, my old friend Eugen, I'm going, I'm leaving you, you need me no longer.

I rose to my feet, tired, wet through and frozen, and I wanted to go and groped for my hat, but I couldn't find it and couldn't remember where I had put it, and while feeling for it on the garden table my hand fell on the book that had lain on it for days or even weeks.

Perhaps it was because I touched the rain-soaked pages, perhaps it was because of a gust of cold air on my face just at the moment when I turned to go, I don't know what it was, but suddenly I felt about me the breath and fragrance of a long-forgotten day, it lasted only for a moment, but for that moment it was resurrected before my eyes and lived for me again. It was an autumn day in the hills outside the city. The smell of withering potato plants floated up to us from the fields. We were walking up the forest track, the green wall of the hill lay ahead of us, and a distant white mist lay over the tree-tops. It lay over the landscape like a premonition of the frost to come, overhead the blue autumn sky was cool and clear, and rose-hip bushes flamed red on both sides of the track.

While we walked Dina rested her head on my shoulder, and the wind played its games with the short brown hair over her brow. Once we stopped and she recited verses about the red leaves of autumn and silver mist lying over the hills.

Then the vision faded as abruptly as it had come. But another memory arose in me. A house high up in the mountains, New Year's Eve, deep snow all round, thick layers of ice on the windows – how good it was that the landlord had put a small iron stove in my room, it crackled and threw up sparks and glowed white-hot. My dog scratched and whined outside the door and wanted to come in. "That's Zamor," I murmured. "Open the door, he won't give me away," Dina murmured, and I freed myself from her lips and arms and opened the door, and for a brief moment a cold draught floated in to us and the clink of glasses and muffled dance music.

Then that vision vanished too, only the feeling of cold remained and the dance music coming from the kitchen window yonder, and inside me there was wild despair and a stabbing pain – how, in God's name, had it come about that we had drifted apart? Was it possible that what had bound two people so closely to each other could disappear? How was it possible that today we had sat opposite each other like two strangers and had nothing to say to each other? How was it possible that she had slipped so suddenly from my arms and that another man should be holding her in his, and that it was now I who was scratching and whining outside the door?

And only then did I realise that that other man was dead, and at that moment I understood for the first time what the word dead really meant.

And I was astounded at the thought that chance had brought it about that I should be here at this day and hour, that I should be on the spot when destiny beckoned. No, it was not chance, it had been foreordained for me, for we are subject to unalterable laws.

And now after this had happened I had wanted to go, to steal away – I could not understand how I had thought of such a thing. And upstairs Dina was sitting in the dark and waiting.

"Is that you, Gottfried? You've been away so long . . ."

"I got up to open the door, darling. You wanted me to. Here I am again."

★

The light was still on in the pavilion. I waited behind a chestnut tree.

The door opened and I heard voices. Felix came out carrying a lantern and walked slowly towards the house.

Two shadows followed behind him. They were Dina and Dr Gorski.

She did not see me.

"Dina," I said softly as she passed very close, nearly touching me with her arm.

She stopped and gripped Dr Gorski's hand.

"Dina," I repeated. She dropped Dr Gorski's hand and took a step towards me.

The lantern glided up the steps and disappeared into the house. For a moment its light enabled me to make out Dina and the shadows of the trees and the bushes and the twining ivy. Then the garden was plunged in darkness again.

I heard Dina's voice from close in front of me.

"Are you still here?" she asked. "What are you doing here?"

Something glided over my forehead like a light, warm hand. I seized it – it was only a withered chestnut leaf falling to the ground.

"I was looking for my dog Zamor," I said quietly, meaning that I had been thinking about old times.

There was a long silence.

Then at last she spoke, quietly and sadly.

"If there's a spark of decency in you," she said, "you will go now, you will go at once."

SIX

I watched her go, and stood there for minutes with nothing in my ears but the sound of the voice that I loved. Not till long after she had gone did I realise the full meaning of what she had said.

At first I was utterly bewildered and dismayed, but this gave way to fury and bitter revolt against the implication of her words, the wrong that was being inflicted on me. Was I to go now? Oh, no, now that was out of the question. My weariness and feverishness had vanished. I was entitled to an explanation, I told myself indignantly, and Felix and Dr Gorski must give me one. Lord knows I had done nothing to her. I had done nothing to her, had I?

Certainly, a misfortune had happened, a terrible misfortune which might perhaps have been prevented. But I was not responsible for it, not I, for heaven's sake. He shouldn't have been left alone, he shouldn't have been left alone for a single minute, how did he get hold of that revolver? And now they seemed to be wanting to put the blame on me. I could understand someone being unfair and not weighing his words at such a moment. But that was just the reason why I must stay, I was entitled to an explanation, I must . . .

Something suddenly occurred to me, something so obvious that it made my agitation seem absurd. Obviously there had been a misunderstanding, it couldn't possibly have been anything else. I had misunderstood what Dina had said, what she had meant had been quite different. All she had meant was that I was to go home, because there was no more that I could do there, that was all, it was as clear as daylight. No-one thought of blaming me in any way. My strained nerves had played a trick on me. Dr Gorski had been there, and had heard everything. I would wait for him, and he would confirm that the whole thing had been merely a misunderstanding.

It won't be long now, I shan't have much longer to wait, I said to myself, Felix and Dr Gorski will soon be back. After all, poor Eugen can't be – they can't leave him alone lying on the floor all night.

I crept to the window as stealthily as a thief in the night and looked into the room. He was still lying on the floor, but he had been covered with a tartan rug. I had seen him once as Macbeth, I couldn't help remembering it. Lady Macbeth's words rang in my ear: "Here's the smell of the blood still. All the perfumes of Arabia . . ."

My teeth started chattering again, and the weariness and the cold sweat and the feverishness came back, but I fought them and drove them away. Rubbish, I said to myself, that quotation was really not appropriate here, and I firmly opened the door and walked in, but this burst of energy promptly faded and gave way to a nervous dread, for now for the first time I was alone with the dead man.

There he lay, completely covered with the rug except for his right hand, which no longer held the revolver. Someone had taken it and put it on the small table in the middle of the room. I went closer to have a look at it, and only then did I notice that I was not alone.

The engineer was standing behind the desk, bending over something I could not see, he seemed to be absorbed in contemplation of the pattern of the wallpaper. He turned when he heard my footsteps.

"So it's you, baron," he said. "What do you look like! Well, this ghastly business has affected you badly."

He stood there, square-shouldered and solidly self-assured, with his hands in his trouser pockets, the very personification of nonchalance, with a cigarette between his lips in a room in which a dead man lay.

"It's the first time you've been confronted with a dead body,

34

isn't it? Lucky you, baron," he said. "You peace-time officers! I thought so at once, because of the gingerly way you walked in. There's no need to watch your step, baron, you won't wake him up."

I said nothing. He confidently threw his cigarette into the ashtray, which was several paces away from him, and immediately lit another.

"I'm a Baltic German, didn't you know that?" he went on. "I was born at Mitau, and I was in the Russo-Japanese war."

"Tsushima?" I asked. I don't know why that naval battle occurred to me, I thought he must have been a ship's engineer or something of the kind.

"No," he said. "The Munho. Ever heard of it?"

I shook my head.

"The Munho. It's not a place but a river. Yellow water winding between the hills. It's better not to think about it. That's where they lay one morning, five hundred of them or more lying side by side, a whole formation of riflemen, with burnt hands and distorted yellow faces. Dreadful, dreadful, there's no other word for it."

"A contact mine?"

"No, high-tension currents. My handiwork. Sometimes when I remember it I say to myself: What of it, it happened in the Far East, five years ago and six thousand miles away, everything that happened there then is now dust and ashes. But it's no good, things like that stick, you don't forget them."

He stopped, and blew a whole series of perfect smoke rings into the air. Anything connected with smoking that he now did suggested a juggling act.

"And now they want to abolish war," he went on after a pause. "They want to abolish war. What good does that do? They want to abolish that and everything else of the kind," he said, pointing to the revolver. "But what good does it do? Human vileness remains, and that's the most lethal of all lethal weapons."

35

Why did he say that to me? I said to myself in surprise and alarm. Does he hold me ultimately responsible for Eugen Bischoff's suicide?

"He voluntarily took his own life," I said quietly.

"Voluntarily?" the engineer exclaimed with a violence that alarmed me. "Are you quite sure of that? Let me tell you something, baron. I was first into this room. The door was locked from the inside, and I smashed the window, the broken glass is still there. I saw his face, I was the first to see his face, and I tell you that the horror on the faces of those five hundred on the Munho river who were climbing the hill in the dark was nothing in comparison with the horror on Eugen Bischoff's face. He had a mad fear of something that is hidden from us, and it was from that fear that he sought escape with the revolver. Went to his death voluntarily? No, baron, Eugen Bischoff was driven to his death."

He lifted the rug and looked at the lifeless face.

"Driven to his death as if with a whip," he then said, with an emotion in his voice which was quite inconsistent with the personality he normally displayed.

I had turned away, because I could not look.

"So, if I have understood you correctly," I said after a while – there was a lump in my throat and talking was an effort – "so you believe, if I have understood you correctly, that he had found out, that somehow or other it had come to his knowledge . . ."

"Found out what? What are you talking about?"

"Presumably you know about the failure of the bank where all his money was?"

"Oh? No, I know nothing about that. This is the first I've heard of it. No, baron, it wasn't that. The fear in his face was of a different kind. Money? No. It had nothing to do with money. You should have seen his face, there's no explanation of that."

After a moment's silence he went on:

"He could still speak when I came in, he said only a few words, I heard them, though they were more breathed than

36

spoken. They were very strange words in the mouth of a dying man . . ."

He paced up and down the room and shook his head.

"They were very strange words. I really knew him so little. One really knows so little about others. You knew him better, or at any rate for longer than I did. Tell me, what was his attitude to religion? I mean, to the Church. Was he religious in your opinion?"

"Religious? He was superstitious, like most stage people. Superstitious in little things. But I never saw in him any sign of faith in the Church meaning of the word."

"All the same, could that fairy tale for credulous children have been his last thought after all?" the engineer said, gazing fixedly at me.

I said nothing, I didn't know what he was talking about, and in any case he was not expecting an answer.

"Never mind," he said to himself with a slight movement of his hand. "That's another thing we shall never get to the bottom of."

He picked up the revolver, which was lying on the table, and looked at it in a way that made it obvious that his mind was on something else. Then he put it back on the table.

"Where did he get that weapon from?" I asked. "Did he own it?"

The engineer awoke as if from a trance.

"The revolver?" he said. "Yes, it was his. Felix says he always had it with him. On his way home at night he had to cross fields and pass building sites where there were plenty of shady characters about. He was nervous of encounters in the dark. The tragedy is that he had the loaded revolver on him. If he'd jumped out of the window – in this case it wouldn't have been serious. A pulled ligament, a sprained ankle, perhaps not even that."

He opened the window and looked out. He stood there for a few seconds, and the wind soughed in the chestnut trees outside and shook and filled the curtains like sails. The papers on the desk fluttered, and a withered chestnut leaf that had strayed into the room darted noiselessly across the floor.

The engineer shut the window and turned to me again.

"He was no coward," he said. "No, by heaven, he was no coward. He didn't make things easy for his killer."

"His killer?"

"Yes, his killer. He was hounded to his death. Look, this is where he stood, and that's where the other man stood."

He pointed to the place on the wall on which he had been concentrating when I came in.

"They stood facing each other," he said slowly, looking at me as he did so. "They stood facing each other eye to eye as in a duel."

Once more I felt uneasy and the lump in my throat returned.

"And who do you think the killer was?"

The engineer looked at me without speaking and slowly, very slowly, shrugged his shoulders.

"Are you still here?" someone suddenly exclaimed in the doorway behind me. "Why don't you go?"

I turned, startled. Dr Gorski was standing in the doorway, and his eyes were on me.

"Go, for heaven's sake," he said. "Go, quickly."

It was too late to go now. It was too late.

Dina's brother appeared behind Dr Gorski, whom he pushed aside and then confronted me.

I looked him in the face. How like his sister he was at that moment. The same strangely shaped oval face and the same spirit of independence in the shape of the lips.

"Are you still here?" he said with an icy politeness that contrasted alarmingly with the doctor's passionate outburst. "I wasn't expecting to find you still here. How very fortunate. That will enable us to clear things up straight away."

SEVEN

I had pulled myself together. It was immediately clear to me when Dina's brother came into the room that I was faced with a mortal enemy, that the confrontation could not be avoided and that the battle must be fought out, though I could not have said at that moment what it was about. All I knew was that I must stay and face up to this enemy whatever the consequences.

Dr Gorski made a last-minute attempt to prevent what was going to happen.

"Felix, please remember where we are," he said, with an imploring and reproachful gesture towards the tartan rug that had been spread over the body. "Must this take place here and now?"

"It's better that it should, what's the point of postponing it, doctor?" Felix replied without taking his eyes off me. "It is really most opportune that Captain von Yosch is still here."

He referred to me, contrary to his usual habit, by my military rank, and I knew what that meant. Dr Gorski stood between us for a moment, undecided. Then he shrugged his shoulders and walked towards the door in order to leave us alone.

But Felix stopped him.

"Please stay, doctor," he said. "A situation could arise in which the presence of a third party might turn out to be useful."

Dr Gorski did not seem immediately to see the point of this observation. He looked at me with an embarrassed expression, as if he wanted to apologise for being a witness of this

39

confrontation. He ended by sitting on the extreme edge of the desk in an attitude that implied that he was ready to leave the room at any moment if anyone wanted him to. Nobody had asked the engineer to stay, but to him this was a plain indication that he too should sit down. He appropriated the only chair in the room, lit a cigarette with a flourish, using only two fingers of his left hand, and acted as if his remaining in the room was a matter of course that needed no justification from any quarter.

I watched all this with a detached and purely objective interest. I was now completely calm and master of my nerves and waited coolly for whatever was going to happen next. For a minute nothing whatever happened. Felix was standing bent over Eugen Bischoff's body, I could not see his face, but it seemed to me that he was struggling with his feelings, as if he were unable to sustain any longer his mask of unnatural calm. For a moment I thought his feelings were about to get the better of him, that he was going to fling himself on the dead body, and that the scene was going to end with that emotional outburst. But nothing of the sort occurred. He straightened up and when he turned to me the expression on his face was one of complete control. I now saw that all he had done was to cover the dead man's head with the rug, which had slipped to the floor.

"Unfortunately we don't have much time," he began, and there was neither grief nor agitation in his voice. "The police commission will be here in about half an hour, and I should like this matter to be settled before they arrive."

"In that our wishes coincide," I said, glancing at the engineer. "The number of witnesses present is completely adequate, in my opinion, as both these gentlemen have been kind enough to put themselves at our disposal."

Dr Gorski moved uneasily on his desk-edge, but the engineer coolly nodded assent.

"Solgrub and Dr Gorski are friends of mine," Felix went on, "and I attach importance to their having as clear as possible a picture of the matter, and I shall not withhold from them any of the circumstances that belong to that picture, including the fact, captain, that four years ago Dina was your mistress."

I was unprepared for this revelation, which took me aback. But my dismay lasted only for a few seconds, and then I had my answer ready.

"I expected to be attacked when I agreed to this discussion, but not to have to listen to slurs directed at a woman of whom I think highly. I cannot permit that, and I must ask you to withdraw the expression that you used . . ."

"Withdraw it, captain? And pray why should I do that, as it coincides in every respect with Dina's view of the matter, of that I can assure you?"

"Am I to understand that your sister authorised you to say that?"

"Yes, captain."

"Then please continue."

A boyish self-conscious smile of satisfaction at the first round having gone so completely in his favour flitted across his lips. But it promptly disappeared, and the tone in which he continued remained unfailingly formal and courteous and even cordial.

"This relationship, on the nature of which we are now in full agreement, lasted for just under six months," he went on. "It ended when you chose to make a trip to Japan. I am saying that it ended, though you for your part no doubt thought of it as a mere interruption . . ."

"I went, not to Japan, but to Tongking and Cambodia," I interrupted. "It was not a pleasure trip, but was on behalf of the Ministry of Agriculture," I added, and behind that correction of entirely unimportant statements of fact, I concealed my amazement at his so easily and indifferently passing over the fact that his sister had been my mistress. What was he getting at? I wondered. If he wanted satisfaction, I was ready and prepared for it. Why did he not come to the point? What else did he have up his sleeve? A slight feeling of anxiety, a premonition of an unknown danger approaching, crept over me and would not let me go.

41

"So you went to Tongking and Cambodia," Felix went on, making a slight gesture of apology with his bandaged hand. "Where you went is in fact irrelevant. But when you came back after about a year you found a changed situation awaiting you for which you were not prepared. Dina had become another man's wife, and you had to face the fact that you had become a stranger to her."

Yes, that had been the situation, and now, as he spoke, the old pain and bitterness of disappointment flared up in me, together with a new feeling I had not had before, hatred of this boy standing in front of me and sticking his finger in things I had kept deeply concealed inside me. Was I accountable to him? Was that why I was here? Was I to stand by while he exposed what had been my secret for years to the inquisitive eyes of others? Enough, enough, I screamed silently, and wanted to attack him and put an end to this scene. But there was this anxiety inside me, the vague and undefined fear of something unknown the threatening closeness of which I could feel – it lay upon me like a nightmare and paralysed me and reduced me to impotence.

Dina's brother went on talking in that completely dispassionate manner of his, and I had to go on listening to him.

"The thought that a woman you believed to be inseparably bound to you had left you and now belonged to another seems to have been intolerable to you. You had suffered your first defeat, you felt challenged, and your supreme objective in life became to win her back. Everything you have done since then, even the most trivial things, served that exclusive purpose."

He paused, perhaps to give me a chance to say something or reply, but I said nothing, and he went on:

"I have been watching you for a long time, for years in fact, watching with passionate interest as if the whole thing were a sporting event or an exciting game of chess, as if it were the race for the Gold Cup and not my sister's happiness that was at stake. I watched you drawing slowly nearer by devious routes, overcoming or evading obstacles, making circles round this house while the circles drew closer and closer. You managed to get yourself sent for, and one day you were there and stood between Dina and her husband."

Now it was coming, the moment was close. I felt my hands trembling in nervous excitement, I couldn't breathe, the silence in the room was so oppressive. It was a relief when Felix started talking again.

"Today I can tell you, captain, that to me the outcome of this battle was never in doubt. You were the stronger, for you had one aim and one aim only, in comparison with which everything else in your life dwindled into insignificance. That made you invincible. To me it was clear that this marriage was going to break up because you wanted it to."

Again he paused, and the fear inside me became unendurable. Perhaps half a minute passed, and my eyes wandered to Dr Gorski – he was leaning against the desk in an attitude of nervous tension, with an expression of utter bewilderment on his face. I could see that no hope was to be expected from him. The engineer was sitting in his armchair in a cloud of cigarette smoke, contemplating his fingertips in bored fashion as if his thoughts were elsewhere.

Felix at last broke the agonising silence.

"That is all over now, and you have lost the game, baron. Your decisive mistake – do you understand what I mean? – Dina will never for one moment tolerate in her presence a man who has her husband's death on his conscience."

So that was it. That was the threat that had been hanging over me and made me tremble. Now that it had been spoken aloud it suddenly struck me as ridiculous and absurd. My confidence returned, my anxiety had vanished. I was faced with an adversary who had fired his shot and missed, and now it was my turn. I felt immensely superior to this boy who had dared to get involved with me. Now I was the stronger, and I knew what to do.

I went up to him, looked him in the eye, and said:

"I hope it has not seriously occurred to you to attribute responsibility for this unhappy event to me or to anyone else?"

This had the effect I expected. He did not sustain my gaze, became embarrassed, and stepped back a pace.

"You surprise me, captain," he replied. "The last thing I expected was that you would deny your part in this. To be quite frank with you, I don't understand you. Aren't you afraid your denial will be wrongly interpreted? Hitherto I have never noticed any lack of courage in you."

"Let us leave the question of my personal courage to a later occasion," I said in a tone that could leave no possible doubt about my ultimate intentions. "In the meantime be kind enough to tell me straight away what role in your opinion I played in this matter."

His embarrassment had been genuine, but by now he had recovered his composure.

"I had hoped you would spare me this, but as you insist, very well," he said. "To put it in a nutshell, you found out, I don't know how, that my brother-in-law had put his savings as well as my sister's small capital in the Bergstein bank, whose failure is reported in today's newspapers. You also knew, or suspected, that Dina wanted to keep this disaster from her husband as long as possible. In your hands knowledge of these two things became a weapon. During the afternoon you repeatedly tried in one way or another to bring the conversation round to the matter. You aimed several times at Eugen, but each time you lowered your weapon when you noticed that Dina and I were watching you. You decided that the opportunity was not good enough, so you waited for a better one. Do I have to go on? When Eugen left the room, you followed him here. At last you were alone with him, there was no-one to help him. You pitilessly told him what we had kept from him. Then you left him, and two minutes later, as you expected, a shot was fired. You had an easy task. You knew he had long since lost belief in himself and his future."

"There were two shots," the engineer said suddenly, but no-one took any notice.

It seemed to me to be time to end this discussion.

"Is that all?" I asked.

Felix did not answer.

"Have you informed Frau Dina of these conjectures of yours?"

"I have talked to my sister about them."

"First of all you will explain to your sister, and today, if you please, that your assumption is wrong. I have nothing to do with any of this. I did not speak to Eugen Bischoff and did not enter this room."

"You didn't enter this room . . . ? No, Dina is no longer here. We took her to my parents half an hour ago. You say you did not enter this room?"

"On my word of honour."

"On your word of honour as an officer?"

"On my word of honour."

"Your word of honour," Felix slowly repeated. He was standing in front of me, bending forward slightly, and he nodded two or three times. Then his attitude changed. He stood erect and stretched, like a man who has successfully completed a hard and troublesome task. For a brief second a smile flitted across his firmly closed lips and vanished again.

"Your word of honour," he said again. "That of course creates a different situation. A word of honour like that greatly simplifies the matter. If you will give me your attention for another moment – an unknown caller left behind something in the room here, something of no particular value which he may perhaps not even have missed yet. Look, here it is."

He had a shiny, reddish-brown object in his bandaged hand. I went nearer, not recognising it at once, and then, horror-stricken, I felt in my jacket pocket for my small English pipe which I always had with me. The pocket was empty.

"It was on the table," Felix went on. "It was there when Dr Gorski and I came in. Look out, doctor!"

Everything started going round and round. Inside me it was dark. It rose in my mind like a long-forgotten memory, as if it had happened years ago. I saw myself walking through the garden, along the gravel path, past the fuchsia beds. Where

45

did the path lead? What did I want in the pavilion? The door creaked when I opened it. How pale Eugen Bischoff went at the first words I whispered, how he looked at the newspaper in dismay and leapt to his feet and then sank back again. And the frightened look that followed me as I left the pavilion and carefully closed the creaking door behind me. There was light on the terrace – that was Dina – I must go up to her – but then – a cry – a shot – down below there was death, and I had summoned it.

"Look out, doctor, he's falling."

No, I was not. I shut my eyes and sat in the armchair.

"It's your pipe, isn't it?"

I nodded. He slowly lowered his white-bandaged hand.

I rose to my feet.

"You want to go, baron?" Felix said. "Well, yes, the matter's settled, and I mustn't take any more of your time. A word of honour, an officer's word of honour, is not one of the things on which we differ and, as we are hardly likely to meet again, I just want to tell you that basically I have never felt hostility to you – never, not even today. I have always had a certain feeling for you, baron. In a strange way I have always felt attracted to you. Liking? No, that would not be the right word. It was more than that – I really am my sister's brother. You are entitled to ask why in spite of such feelings I have put you in a situation in which, as matters stand at present, there is only one way out for you. Well, one can gaze in fascination at a wild cat or a pine-marten, one can be captivated by the grace of the creature's posture and movements and the boldness of its leaps, and yet shoot it down in cold blood because it is a beast of prey. It remains for me to assure you that you are under no obligation whatever to carry out in the next twenty-four hours the decision that you have no doubt already made. I shall in no circumstances inform the court of honour of your regiment of this business, should that step turn out to be necessary, before the end of the week. That is the only thing I still wanted to tell you."

★

I heard all this, but my mind was on the dark muzzle of the revolver that lay on the table. I saw it with two big round eyes staring into my own, coming closer and closer and getting bigger and bigger and swallowing up the whole room, and I could see nothing else at all.

Suddenly I heard the engineer's voice. "You are doing the baron a grave wrong," he said. "He had as little to do with the murder as you or I had."

EIGHT

I have only an indistinct memory of the moment when my head cleared again. I heard myself sighing deeply; it was the first sound that broke the silence of the room. Then I became aware of a slight gnawing sensation in my head. It was not really painful, and the discomfort soon went away.

The first feeling I can describe was one of amazement. What had I landed myself in? What was it, what madness had seized me and held me in its grip? Then a feeling of depression took over.

How is it possible, I asked myself in astonishment and alarm. I had seen myself walking into this room, heard myself whispering words I never spoke. I myself believed in my own guilt. How can that be possible? A hallucination, a waking dream had led me astray. A strange will had tried to force me to confess a crime I did not commit. No, I had not been here, I did not talk to Eugen Bischoff, I am not a murderer. All that had been dream and illusion that had risen from hell and had now been banished.

I breathed again in liberation and relief. I had not given in, but had fought back. The inexplicable power that had weighed down on me had been broken. Inside me and all round me everything had changed, and I had returned to the world of reality.

I looked up and saw Felix towering over me. The same obstinate hostility was still on his lips. He seemed determined not to be deprived of his victory, and he turned and angrily faced the engineer as if he were a new and dangerous enemy. He glared at him irritably from beneath knitted brows as if ready to assault him, and he raised his bandaged hand in a gesture of furious surprise that failed to intimidate the engineer.

"Calm yourself, Felix," said he. "I know exactly what I'm saying. I have considered it very carefully, and have come to the conclusion that the baron is innocent. You have done him a grave wrong, and all I ask is that you should listen to me, that's all."

The assurance with which he spoke had a calming effect on my nerves. I had a feeling of liberation, the nightmare that had oppressed me a moment before had been dissipated. The idea that I had been seriously accused of murder now struck me as fantastic and absurd. Now that broad daylight, the light of reality, had begun to illuminate things, what I felt was merely a kind of tension that might be felt by an uninvolved spectator. All I felt was curiosity. How would it all turn out, I wondered. Who drove Eugen Bischoff to his death? Who is the guilty party? And by what strange concatenation of circumstances did that silent witness, my pipe, arrive in the room and end up on the table? At whom did it point the finger of suspicion?

That was what I wanted to know, that was what I had to find out, and I kept my eyes on the engineer, as if he knew the way out of this maze of unsolved riddles.

I don't know what was uppermost in my enemy's mind at that moment. Anger? Impatience? Irritation? Indignation or disappointment? Whatever it was, he managed to hide it. His face and manner expressed the same courtesy and cordiality as before, and the angry movement of his hand turned into a moderate, challenging gesture.

"You intrigue me, Waldemar," he said. "Let us hear what you have to say. But you'll be brief, won't you, because I think I can hear the police commission car."

Sure enough, there was honking outside in the street, but the engineer took no notice, and when he began speaking I remembered for a brief moment that my honour and my life were at stake. But the feeling of calm and confidence and

49

complete non-involvement promptly returned, together with the conviction that the whole thing would turn out to have its natural explanation. It had become inconceivable to me that this dreadful suspicion could stick to me.

"When the shots rang out, Baron von Yosch was up in the house, wasn't he?" the engineer said. "Did you know that? He was on the terrace, talking to your sister. That must be our starting point."

"That may well be," Felix said in the tone in which one discusses trivialities. He was still listening to what was going on outside, but the honking had faded into the distance.

"It is an important point which we must bear in mind," the engineer went on, "for I have reason to believe that Eugen Bischoff's unknown visitor was still in the room here when the two shots were fired."

"Two shots? I heard only one."

"There were two. I haven't examined the revolver yet, but you will find that I am right."

He went over to the wall and pointed to the pale blue flowers and leaves and scrollwork of the pattern of the wallpaper.

"That's where the bullet went in," he said. "He tried to defend himself, Felix. He fired at his adversary and then turned the weapon against himself. That is what happened. At the critical moment the baron was up on the terrace. When we look for the unknown visitor he won't come into it, that's certain."

Dr Gorski bent over to the hole in the wallpaper and sought for the bullet with his pocket knife. I listened to the sound of his knife scratching the plaster. Felix was still listening to what was going on in the street.

"Is that so certain?" Dr Gorski said after a while without turning his head. "How did the unknown visitor get into the garden, can you tell me that? No-one saw him or heard the bell being rung. I know what you're going to say, your mysterious stranger had a spare key to the garden door, didn't he?"

The engineer shook his head.

"No. I rather think he had been waiting for Eugen Bischoff here in the pavilion for a long time, perhaps for hours."

"Oh? Then will you explain to me how he left the room? You say he was here when the first shot was fired. But there was only a second between the two shots, and when we arrived the door was bolted from the inside."

"I've given a great deal of thought to that," the engineer said with no trace of embarrassment. "The windows were shut too. I gladly admit that this is a weak point in my argument, so far the only one that might incriminate the baron."

"The only one?" exclaimed Felix. "What about his pipe? Who brought that English pipe here? Your mysterious visitor, or perhaps even Eugen himself?"

"At all events I would not exclude the second possibility," the engineer said.

Felix had an expletive ready on his lips, but Dr Gorski, who had been listening in silence, spoke first.

"I'm not sure, I might be mistaken," he said, "but I think I really saw the pipe for a moment in Eugen Bischoff's hand. As I said, I might be mistaken . . ."

"Really, doctor?" Felix interrupted. "Do you remember having ever seen my brother-in-law smoking? No, doctor, he didn't smoke, he hated it . . ."

"I'm not saying he intended to smoke it," Dr Gorski interrupted. "He may merely have taken the pipe with him because he was holding it in his hand. Look, I myself once absent-mindedly walked out into the street with a big pair of scissors in my hand, and if I hadn't met some friends . . ."

"No, doctor, you should take the trouble to look for plausible hypotheses. The pipe was still glowing when I came in. Look, there are still half-a-dozen burnt matchsticks on the floor. Someone had been smoking that pipe."

Dr Gorski had no answer to that, but the effect of those words on the engineer is hard to describe.

He jumped to his feet. Suddenly he was white as chalk. He stared at us one after the other and then cried:

"So the pipe was still smouldering. That's it, then. Don't

51

you remember, Felix? There was a cigarette still alight on the desk."

Not one of us suspected where his train of thought had led him. What struck me most was that in his excitement he had spoken with a marked Slavonic accent. We looked at each other with surprise at the way he stood there, quite pale and beside himself, unable to speak clearly or explain but only to stammer, and at the same time having to fight a fit of anger, so that at first we were unable to grasp what he was trying to say.

Felix shook his head.

"You must be clearer, Waldemar," he said, "I haven't understood a word."

"And I was the first in the room," the engineer exclaimed. "Where the devil were my eyes? Be clearer? As if it weren't clear enough. He shut himself up in the room and bolted the door and when the landlady went in there was a burning cigarette on his desk. Do you understand now, or don't you want to understand?"

At last I realised what he was talking about. I had thought no more about the mysterious suicide of the naval officer who had been a friend of Eugen Bischoff's. With a slight shudder I realised the resemblance of the two cases, and the dark and alarming suspicion of a connection between them rose in me for the first time.

"The same external circumstances and the same course of events," the engineer said, drawing his hand across his furrowed brow. "Practically the same course of events, besides the total absence of any discernible motive in all three cases."

"And what conclusions do you draw from that?" asked Felix, disconcerted and not quite so sure of his case.

"Above all, that Baron von Yosch is completely innocent. Isn't that clear to you at last?"

"And whom do you suspect, Waldemar?"

The engineer took a long look at the body that lay covered on the floor, and for some strange reason he dropped his voice. Softly, almost in a whisper, he said:

"When he told us about his friend's fate he may have been only a step away from the solution of the mystery. He suspected it when he left the room, that's why he was so agitated, he was quite beside himself, don't you remember?"

"Well? Go on."

"That young naval officer went to his death after he hit on the reason for his brother's suicide. Eugen guessed the reason too. Perhaps that was why he too had to die . . ."

The quiet was broken by the ringing of the garden doorbell. Dr Gorski opened the door and looked out. We heard voices.

Felix raised his head. His expression had changed. He had recovered his composure.

"The police commission," he said in an entirely altered tone. "Waldemar," he said, "you obviously don't realise into what realms of fantasy you have soared. No, your theories don't hold water. You must excuse me now, I want to talk to these gentlemen alone."

He went over to Dr Gorski and shook his hand warmly.

"Good night, doctor," he said. "I shall never forget what you did today for Dina and me. What would we have done without you? You thought of everything. You kept your head, doctor."

Then he turned to me.

"I must again assure you, captain," he said casually, "that nothing has changed in this affair. Our agreement stands, doesn't it?"

I bowed silently.

NINE

The rest of what happened at Eugen Bischoff's villa that evening can be quickly told.

As we walked through the garden we met the police commission, which consisted of three gentlemen in civilian clothes, one of whom had a big brown leather briefcase under his arm. The deaf gardener led the way with his lantern. We stood aside to let them pass, and one of them, an elderly gentleman with a full face and a grey moustache – he was the district medical officer, as it turned out – stopped and exchanged a few words with Dr Gorski.

"Good evening, my dear colleague," he said, holding his briefcase in front of his face. "Rather cold for the time of year, isn't it? Were you called in?"

"No, I happened to be here."

"What's it all about? We know nothing yet."

"I don't want to anticipate your findings," Dr Gorski replied evasively, and as I walked on I didn't hear the rest of the conversation.

No-one seemed to have entered the music room since I had left it. The chair that had been knocked over was still in the doorway, my score sheets were scattered all over the floor, and Dina's shawl still hung over the back of a chair.

A cold, damp night wind came in through the open window, and I shivered as I buttoned up my jacket. As I bent to pick up the music my eyes fell on a sheet that bore the title "Trio in B major, Op. 8", and I felt as if we had only just finished the scherzo, and the final chords on the piano and the long-drawn-out final passage on the cello rang in my ear. An agreeable vision enabled me to imagine we were still sitting round the tea table, that nothing had happened, that the engineer was blowing blue smoke rings into the air, that Dina's even breathing was coming from the piano, and that Eugen Bischoff was pacing slowly up and down accompanied by his shadow gliding noiselessly across the carpet.

I started suddenly when a door slammed. I heard loud voices in the ante-room, my name was mentioned, the engineer and the doctor were talking about me, they seemed to think I had long since gone home.

"I could credit him with anything," I heard the doctor say emphatically, "there's no act of violence or wickedness I think him incapable of – good gracious, it's half past ten already – I even think him capable of murder, it wouldn't be his first. But lying on his word of honour? No."

"It wouldn't be his first?" said the engineer. "What do you mean by that?"

"Good gracious, he's a cavalry officer, isn't he? Am I to give you my views on duelling standing here in this draught? He's capable of ruthlessness to the point of brutality, I could tell you a tale about that – your overcoat's hanging on the rack over there – he can be in love with a horse or a dog, but I assure you that the life of a human being who stands in his way doesn't mean very much to him."

"I think you're quite wrong about him. My impression . . ."

"Listen just a minute, I know him – wait a moment – I've known him for fifteen years . . ."

"But I know a little about human nature, too. He has never given me the impression of ruthlessness or brutality. On the contrary, he strikes me as a very sensitive individual, living only for his music, a basically shy and retiring . . ."

"My dear engineer, which of us can be summed up in a few simple characteristics? You can't sum up the whole character of a human being in a few catch-phrases. Human character is not such a simple thing as one of your green bobbins, charged with either positive or negative electricity. It may be perfectly true that he's sensitive or over-sensitive, and he may be shy and retiring, but there's room for plenty of other things too, believe me."

I was standing bent over a sheet of music and I dared not move, as the door was ajar and the slightest movement might betray my presence. I wasn't interested in their discussion, all I wanted was that they should go away as quickly as possible, for having to play the eavesdropper was painful to me. But they went on talking, and I had to listen, whether I wanted to or not.

"But telling a lie on his word of honour, no," the doctor said. "There are inner moral imperatives that even the greatest cynic does not infringe. Social status, family tradition, sense of honour – no, a Baron von Yosch does not tell a lie on his word of honour. Felix is wrong."

"Felix is wrong," the engineer repeated. "That was obvious to me from the first moment. We find an old trail, and instead of following it right back to its source, instead of taking the most obvious course, the course that lies nearest to hand . . ."

"What on earth has the baron to do with the suicide of that Academy student? That's a question Felix ought to have asked . . . Eugen Bischoff is dead, I still can't grasp the fact."

"We'll get to the bottom of it, doctor, it's our duty. Are you willing to help me?"

"Help you? What can we do except to let things take their course?"

"Oh? Let things take their course?" the engineer exclaimed loudly and excitedly. "No, doctor, that's something I've never done in my life. To me letting things take their course has always been the most loathsome of the disguises assumed by sloth. Letting things take their course means saying: I'm too stupid, too lazy or too heartless . . ."

"Thank you," said Dr Gorski. "You really are a good judge of human nature."

"Perhaps, doctor. You see, the baron whom you call a ruthless man of action, a man without conscience or inhibitions –

believe me, doctor, he strikes me as being like one of our Russian borzois. Do you know the breed? Slender, proud, not very active mentally, but thoroughly aristocratic, they look as if you ought to be wary of them, though actually if their life is threatened in any way they are utterly helpless. We must think for him, doctor. Do you really propose to leave him in the lurch? If things are left to take their course, they'll inevitably turn against him, and at the end of that road there's the revolver, bear that in mind. Haven't there been enough sacrifices, doctor?"

Dr Gorski did not answer. For a whole minute I heard him rummaging about, and then something crashed to the floor. This was followed by some angry muttering, which gave way to a series of very expressive curses.

"What are you looking for?" asked the engineer.

"My stick, where on earth did I leave it? The worst of it is that it isn't mine, it's my caretaker's. Here's my rheumatism again. I should have gone to Pistyan for the waters a long time ago. It's a brown stick with a thick horn handle, have you seen it anywhere?"

This alarmed me, because a brown stick with a horn handle was leaning against the wall next to the fireplace.

I had been hoping that the two of them would go away without noticing me, but there was no hope of that now, for the doctor was bound to come and look for his stick here. So I had to anticipate him.

I rose and casually dropped the music sheets on the table. Then I went to the piano and noisily shut the lid of the violin case. Let the two of them realise that I was there and had heard every word of their careless talk.

Dr Gorski's angry muttering stopped immediately, and all I could hear was the ticking of the clock; no doubt the two were looking aghast at each other. I imagined their dismayed and embarrassed faces, and for a moment I vividly pictured the doctor, a gnome turned into a Biblical pillar of salt in his caped cloak and galoshes.

Eventually they seemed to regain the power of speech.

Excited whispering began, and then I heard the engineer's firm and energetic footsteps.

I went to meet him very casually indeed, for the situation was far more embarrassing for him than for me. I was just about to open the door when the telephone rang next to me.

Quite automatically I picked up the receiver. It did not occur to me until later that the call could not possibly have been for me.

"Hallo," I said.

"Who's there?" said the voice at the other end of the line. It was a voice that I knew; I immediately had the impression that I was talking to a quite young girl, and that idea was associated with the memory of a strange perfume, the odour of ether or ethereal oils. For a second I wondered where I had heard that voice before.

The lady on the line became impatient.

"To whom am I speaking?" she said irritably, and I became confused, because the door had been pushed open and the engineer was standing in the doorway in his overcoat and with his hat in his hand. He looked at me inquiringly.

"This is the Bischoff villa," I said eventually.

"There's my stick," Dr Gorski exclaimed with great satisfaction. He had forced his way past the engineer in the doorway and was standing in the room rubbing his leg.

"Is the professor there?" asked the lady on the telephone.

"The professor?" I could not think whom she meant. My first thought was that it was a wrong number, and I remembered that Dina had once complained that her number was always being confused with that of the senior registrar at the eye hospital.

"Here it goes again," the doctor complained. "What I need is a couple of weeks of sulphur baths but, believe it or not, this summer I couldn't manage that even once."

"Whom do you want?" I asked.

"Professor Bischoff, Eugen Bischoff."

I now remembered that Eugen Bischoff taught drama at the Academy of Interpretive Arts. It was extraordinary that I had not thought of that before. Presumably this was one of his pupils, but I could not explain why her voice reminded me of the smell of ether.

"The professor is not available," I said to her.

"For heaven's sake hurry up," Dr Gorski said to the engineer. "How much longer am I to wait in this draught with my rheumatism?"

"Oh, stop it, the clothes rack fell on your shin, that's what your rheumatism is," the engineer whispered to him.

"Nonsense," Dr Gorski exclaimed angrily. "What nonsense you talk. I ought to know what muscle pains are."

"Not available? Not even for me?" the lady said in a very self-assured manner – she seemed to think it quite unnecessary to mention her name. "Not even for me? But he's expecting me to call."

This nonplussed me, and Dr Gorski's continual interruptions increased my confusion. What was I to say to her?

"I'm afraid the professor is not available to anyone," I replied, and suddenly remembered the tartan rug and the pallid face that it covered – a cold shudder went down my spine and my hands trembled.

"Not available to anyone?" said the voice on the telephone in a tone of surprise and disbelief. "But he's expecting my call."

"Look, I think it's raining again," said the doctor. "It'll be the death of me. No chance of getting a cab, I know that already."

"For heaven's sake keep quiet for a minute," the engineer told him abruptly.

"What's the meaning of this? Has there been an accident?" the voice on the telephone exclaimed.

"The pain's in the side and the back too, this is a fine kettle of fish," the doctor, now completely cowed, whispered. Then he fell silent.

"What has happened? Tell me, for heaven's sake," the voice on the telephone said.

"Nothing. Nothing at all," I answered, and the question:

how can she possibly know, where can she have got it from? flashed through my mind. No, no-one would find out from me, only Felix had the right . . . "Nothing has happened," I said, trying to make my voice sound completely natural, but the staring eyes in the pale, distorted face would not go away. "The professor has retired to work, that's all," I said.

"To work? Oh, good gracious me, the new role, of course. And I thought . . . What a stupid idea. I was afraid . . ."

She laughed quietly to herself. Then she went on in the same self-assured tone as before:

"I wouldn't want to disturb the professor, of course. May I ask whom I'm speaking to?"

"Baron von Yosch."

"Don't know you, I'm afraid," she answered very decidedly, and again I had the feeling that I had heard that voice more than once before, though I still had no idea when and where. "Will you please be kind enough to tell the professor – he should have called on me this afternoon, but suddenly, at midday, he put me off. Please tell him that I expect him at eleven o'clock tomorrow morning. Tell him that everything's ready, and, in case he has no time again tomorrow, tell him I'm not in the mood to postpone the matter again."

"And whom am I to say this message is from?"

"Tell him," and now the voice was very ill-humoured, like that of a spoilt child who has failed to get something it wanted, "tell the professor that in no circumstances am I prepared to wait any longer for the Day of Judgment. That's all."

"The Day of Judgment?" I said in surprise and with a feeling of slight discomfort for which I had no explanation.

"Yes, the Day of Judgment," she said emphatically. "Please give the professor that message. Thank you."

I heard her ring off and I put back the receiver. At the same moment I felt my shoulder being grabbed. I turned my head – the engineer was standing beside me staring me in the face.

"What was that?" he stammered. "What was it you just said?"

60

"It wasn't me, it was a lady, the lady on the telephone, she said she wouldn't wait any longer for the Day of Judgment."

He let me go and grabbed the receiver. His hat had dropped to the floor. I picked it up.

"It's too late, she has rung off."

He slammed down the receiver.

"Whom were you talking to?"

"Whom? I don't know. She wouldn't give her name. But I thought I knew her voice. That's all I can tell you."

"Try and remember," he yelled at me. "For heaven's sake try and remember. I must find out whom you were talking to. You've got to remember, do you hear? You've got to remember."

I shrugged my shoulders.

"If you like I'll ring the exchange," I said. "Perhaps they'll be able to tell me where the call came from."

"That's quite hopeless, don't waste your time, try and remember instead. She asked for Eugen Bischoff. What did she want from him?"

I repeated the conversation word for word for his benefit.

"You too find it strange, don't you?" I said to him when I had finished. "The Day of Judgment? What can be the meaning of that?"

"I don't know," he replied, gazing at the floor. "All I know is that those were Eugen Bischoff's last words."

We stood silently facing each other.

Nothing moved in the room, there was no sound but the ticking of the clock, until Dr Gorski, who had been looking out into the garden, shut the window.

"Thank God, it has stopped raining," he said.

"What the hell do I care whether it's raining or not?" the engineer exclaimed in a sudden fit of fury. "Don't you understand? Someone's life's in danger."

"You're worrying about me quite unnecessarily," I said to calm him. "I'm not really as helpless as you seem to assume, and besides . . ."

He looked at me blankly. Then he noticed his hat, and took it from me.

"It's not your life that's at risk," he said. "No, not yours."

Then he walked out, walked out like a sleep-walker. He walked down the stairs and out, his crushed hat in his hand, without saying goodbye and taking no notice of Dr Gorski or me.

TEN

As I made my way home through the brightly lit streets that
evening, hatless, in a state of great agitation, and with a gash
on my forehead, the impression I must have made on passers-
by was that I had gone out of my mind. I have never found
out how I got the gash, but it probably happened in the
pavilion when I lost consciousness for a few seconds – it was
only a slight attack of weakness that passed off quickly – my
forehead must have come into contact with something hard,
the arm of a chair or the edge of the desk. I distinctly remember
that soon afterwards I felt a sharp, penetrating pain over my
right eye. As it passed off so quickly I took no more notice of
it. Out in the street I still knew nothing about the gash, and
the look of surprise on the faces of people I passed put a strange
idea into my head.

It seemed to me that the whole town knew what had just
happened at the Bischoff villa, was taking a passionate interest
in the affair, knew me and regarded me as the murderer.

The look of amazement on the face of a student emerging
from a night café seemed to say: Is it possible that he hasn't
been arrested yet? This alarmed me, and I pressed on. Two
sisters were waiting to be let in outside the door of some flats,
and there could be no possible doubt that one of them, the
one with a branch of a rowan tree in her hand, recognised
me. "There he is," she whispered, and turned away with a
look of indignation and horror. She had a pale face, and I
caught a glimpse of red hair under the broad brim of her
summer hat.

Then an old gentleman with twitching hands stopped and

looked at me concernedly, and actually seemed about to talk to me. How could you harry the poor man to death, he seemed to be going to say, how could you do such a thing?

That's enough, damn it, was the thought that flashed through my mind, and he realised that if he said anything I'd take him by the throat, and that frightened him and he made off.

The next thing that happened robbed me of the last remnants of my self-control.

A cyclist, a big, muscular fellow with bare arms and a brutal expression, he looked like a baker's assistant in his string vest, approached silently, dismounted right in front of me and glared at me.

He's looking for you, he's after you, I said to myself, and I ran across the street, and went on running until I came to my senses and stopped, panting, in a dark side-street a long way out of my way.

I felt frightened and ashamed of myself. What came over me, what was I running away from? Was it conceivable that the whole town should be in a state of shock because one man had shot himself? What craziness to read Felix's senseless accusations in the eyes and behaviour of indifferent strangers whom chance put in my path. I had allowed a figment of the imagination to terrify me.

I've had enough, I'm going home, I whispered angrily to myself. It's my nerves, I must take some bromine when I get back. I've had too much for one day. What have I to be afraid of? I have no responsibility for what happened. I could not have prevented it, no-one could have prevented it. I have nothing and no-one to fear, I can quietly go on my way, I can look people in the face as calmly as I did yesterday and every other day.

And yet something inside me made me make wide circles round everyone coming towards me. I went round the ring of bright light under the gas lamps, and I started when I heard footsteps behind me. At a street corner I heard a cab slowly passing by. I hailed it, it stopped, and a sleepy cabbie drove me home.

By the time I opened the door of my flat I had made up my mind to go away. My nerves are shattered, I mumbled to myself as I walked in. I repeated this five or six times, and when I caught myself at it I was horrified. Yes, I must get out of here. But not to the Mediterranean, not to Nice, Rapallo or the Lido. I had an estate in Bohemia, in the Chrudim area, which had been left to me by a cousin on my mother's side who died young. I had spent part of my boyhood in the old manor house, and checking through the regular accounts, the reports and proposals sent me by my manager there always reminded me of long past summers. Since then I had been there only once, when I spent a week shooting roebuck in the Chrudim woods. That had been five years ago.

That was where I would go now. That was where I should find the peace and solitude that I needed as never before in my life. It did not occur to me at the time that in Vienna my disappearance might be wrongly interpreted as flight, a confession of guilt, a desperate attempt to extricate myself from a net of irrefutable evidence. I wanted to get away from the city, that was all, and I imagined myself spending the next few weeks wandering for hours uphill and downhill through the endless pinewoods, making friends with a shaggy old hunting dog, revisiting the pool where as a boy looking for sea monsters I had caught water-beetles, newts and leeches, spending a Sunday afternoon at the village inn among taciturn Czech peasants and card-playing foresters, and spending an hour before going to bed in the evening in an armchair in front of a blazing wood fire with books, a bottle of red wine, and my pipe.

That was the life I envisaged for myself for the next few weeks, and no sooner had I made my plans than I wanted to put them into practice. I paced up and down the room, burning with impatience, wishing I were already in the train and hating all the familiar things that met my eyes, the desk, the brightly coloured Gobelin curtains, the Albanian arquebus and the green silk prayer mat on the wall.

The fever of impatience I was in made idle waiting impossible, so, to confirm my decision inside myself as well as for the sake of doing something that would bring the carrying out of my plan nearer, I fetched my two suitcases and started packing, as if there were no time to lose. In spite of my restlessness, I set about it methodically and thought of everything – even my man Vinzenz could not have done better. I even remembered the small pocket compass and the German-Czech dictionary that I had taken with me on my trip to Bohemia five years before. When I had finished, and the place was littered with books, articles of clothing, leather spats and washing, and I locked the suitcases, I started thinking about the other things I should have to do before I left. First of all I should have to go to the bank to get some money. Then I must have a talk with my lawyer – I would telephone him and ask him to come and see me. Leave? No, my leave had not expired yet. I had an appointment to dine with friends at the Opera restaurant on Wednesday evening, and I must put them off, and I must send a telegram to my estate manager asking him to send the car to meet me at the station. There were also a few bills and a gaming debt to settle – I wanted to leave all my affairs in order. There was some last-minute shopping to do in town, and then there was the Count Wenckheim Memorial Tournament at the fencing club for which I had entered my name – a few lines to the secretary would settle that.

That was all I could think of at the moment, and I wrote it all down and put the note under the paper-weight on the desk. My restlessness diminished slightly. I had done all I could do at this late hour to get ready for my departure. It was five minutes past two – time to go to bed.

But I was still too agitated to be able to sleep. For a time I lay with closed eyes, but no trace of tiredness made its appearance, and my over-active mind was in turmoil with a hundred alarming ideas. I remembered the sleeping tablets on my bedside table. Only two small bromine tablets were left in the box, and I took them both.

I would have to buy bromine or morphine drops or veronal or some sort of drug in the morning – I mustn't forget. I'd need something of the sort in the days to come, I said to myself, and I jumped out of bed and started anxiously looking for the prescription, first in my briefcase, then in all the drawers of the desk and all the corners of the cupboards and chests-of-drawers and finally in my jacket pockets, but it was nowhere to be found.

Never mind, I don't need it, I said to myself. They know me at the Archangel pharmacy across the road, the proprietor greets me when I pass, he'll let me have a little bromine without a prescription. I mustn't forget it, or I'll have a sleepless journey tomorrow.

I fetched the notes I had made for next morning and, as I wrote the word bromine, without being aware of any connection, I suddenly remembered the voice on the telephone, the voice of the woman who had been unwilling to wait for the Day of Judgment. How strange that sounded. At the same time I remembered what the engineer had said. "Try and remember. For heaven's sake try and remember." Yes, now that I had time and peace to do so, I must try and remember. I must not go to sleep, but must try and remember when and where I had heard that voice. It was now clear to me that that unknown woman possessed the key to the mystery and could tell us why Eugen Bischoff had died; she knew, and I must find her and talk to her . . .

I lay in bed and pressed my hands to my temples and tried to recall the sound of her voice in my ears, but it would not come. The sleeping tablets began to have their effect.

A feeling of tiredness crept over me, and all that had happened now struck me as unreal and strangely unsubstantial, a play of shadows on the wall. I was still awake, but already I felt the soothing hand of sleep. Disconnected, meaningless words, harbingers of a coming dream, sounded in my ear – it's still raining, a voice said, and other voices mingled with it, and I started awake and was alone. A fly buzzed through the room, and down in the street a man went by and tapped the pavement once, twice, three times with his stick. I heard it, but at the same time it seemed to me that somewhere in the distance a woodpecker was hammering. Pinewoods soughed in the wind, the cry of a bird came from a long way away, once more I tried to open my eyes, and then that day came to an end.

ELEVEN

Vinzenz, standing at the bedside with my breakfast, woke me. The room was dark, all I could make out was his outline and a faint gleam from the silver milk jug. He said something, but I could not make out what he said. I wanted to go back to sleep and resisted waking up. I felt vaguely afraid of getting up and facing another day.

"What's the time?" I asked, and must have dropped off to sleep again, but not for long, perhaps only for a few seconds, because when I opened my eyes Vinzenz was still standing by my bed.

"It's past nine o'clock, sir," I heard him say.

"Impossible," I replied. "It's pitch dark."

I heard the gentle rattle of the breakfast things and foot-steps shuffling across the carpet, the shutters were drawn, daylight flooded into the room and there was a painful light in my eyes.

"If you're going away, sir, it's high time you got up, if I may say so, sir," Vinzenz said from just by the window.

"Going away? Where? Why?" I asked, still half asleep. I tried to think, but all I could remember was that overnight I had packed my two suitcases. "There's plenty of time. I want you to take the luggage to the station."

"To the South Station?"

It took me quite a time to remember where I was going.

"No, I'm going to Chrudim. Let down the shutters, I want to go to sleep again."

"Good heavens!" Vinzenz suddenly exclaimed. "What do you look like, sir?"

"What's the matter now?" I said irritably and sat up in bed.

"Your forehead, sir, just over the right eye. Where did you get that, sir?"

I felt my brow.

"Let me see," I said, and Vinzenz brought me the mirror.

The sight of the gash and the dried blood surprised me, and I could not explain how I had got it.

"The staircase was not lit again last night," I said just for the sake of dismissing the subject. "Now go and let me sleep."

"And what shall I tell the gentleman, sir? He's waiting, and says it's urgent."

"What gentleman, for heaven's sake?"

"I've already told you, sir. There's a gentleman in the other room, a tall, fair gentleman who has never been here before. He says it's essential that he should talk to you, sir, and he has made himself comfortable at the desk, just as if he were at home here, sir."

"Did he mention his name?"

"His card is on the sugar bowl, sir."

I picked up the card. The name on it was Waldemar Solgrub. I read it two or three times before remembering the events of the previous day. This made me feel uncomfortable. What could the engineer be wanting at this time of day? It certainly boded nothing good. I wondered whether to excuse myself on the grounds of indisposition or simply say I was not at home. I wanted to be alone, I didn't want to see anyone or be told anything.

That was my first reaction, but I changed my mind.

"I'll have breakfast later," I told Vinzenz. "Ask the gentleman to be patient for a little while longer. Tell him I'll be with him in five minutes."

The engineer was sitting at my desk when I went in. He looked tired, as if he had been up all night. There were five or six cigarette stubs in the ashtray in front of him, obviously he had chain-smoked while waiting for me. He was holding his head in his hands and staring into the void with a curiously glazed

70

expression. His lower lip was slightly twisted, as if he were in physical pain, but that expression vanished from his face as soon as he was aware of my presence. He rose and approached me. There was a look of eager expectation in his eyes.

"You must forgive me for disturbing you so early," he began, "but I really could not wait any longer."

"No, I'm obliged to you," I replied. "Contrary to my usual habit, I slept much too long. Would you like a cup of tea?"

"That's very kind of you, no tea, thank you, but if I may be so bold, a little brandy . . . Thank you, that's enough. Well, you know why I'm here."

"I assume Felix sent you," I replied. "Has anything new happened since yesterday?"

"No, not yet. Nothing new has happened so far," he muttered, and that glazed look reappeared in his eyes.

"Then at the moment I really don't know . . ."

"I'm afraid I've disturbed you for nothing," he said. He sat leaning forward, looking past me with an entirely expressionless face. "I imagined you would be able to tell me to whom you talked on the telephone about Eugen Bischoff yesterday, you remember? You haven't thought any more about who the lady was?"

"Yes, I have," I said hurriedly, and as I spoke I had a kind of inspiration. I suddenly reached a conclusion that struck me as convincing and irrefutable. "I have been thinking about it, and I have decided that the lady to whom I talked can only be an actress whom I must have seen on the stage, for Eugen Bischoff and I had few friends and acquaintances in common. But unfortunately I have so far failed to remember when and in what play or plays I have seen her."

"Thank you," the engineer said briefly, staring blankly at the green silk prayer mat on the wall.

"I think the name will occur to me, but you must give me time," I went on after a while. "Not too many people come into it, because recently I haven't been going to the theatre very much."

The engineer sat listlessly facing me, resting his head on his hand. He still said nothing, and his silence became intolerable to me.

"Supposing we met again this afternoon," I suggested, "say about five o'clock, if you'll allow me the time, I'm sure that by then . . ."

He interrupted me with a gesture.

"No, don't trouble yourself any further," he said, and suddenly asked for the brandy bottle and started drinking one glass after another like a maniac.

"At five o'clock this afternoon, you said," he went on after about the seventh glass. "At five o'clock this afternoon I shall know to whom you talked yesterday. As the situation is at present, there's no possible doubt about it."

"Really?" I exclaimed in incredulous surprise. "Have you a clue, then? Honestly, I can't imagine how . . ."

"I know what I'm saying, you can depend on it," the engineer muttered, and helped himself to yet another glass of brandy and then a second and a third, he seemed to be used to drinking brandy by the tumblerful.

"It would naturally be extremely important to find out who the lady is," I said. "I think we have some questions to put to her, don't you think so? Particularly . . ."

He shook his head.

"I don't think we'll get anything from her," he said and relapsed into his brooding silence.

A few minutes passed while we sat silently facing each other. In my bedroom Vinzenz was muttering to himself as usual. Sometimes he interrupted himself to hum the refrain of some Styrian soldier's song. Muffled street noises were audible through the open window, a passing lorry made the teacups, the brandy glasses and the silver milk jug rattle. I noticed on the desk the notes I had jotted down the night before, and I picked them up and put them in my pocket.

The engineer suddenly rose to his feet. He paced very energetically up and down the room several times and stopped in front of my suitcases.

"So that settles that," he said in completely different tones.

"I'm sorry to have disturbed your sleep. It was really quite unnecessary. I see you're going away."

"Yes, to Bohemia. I have a small estate near Chrudim. Another brandy? I'm taking the seven o'clock train this evening."

"May I ask what has persuaded you to leave here so suddenly?"

"Roebuck that are waiting to be shot, that's all."

"Do you think the roebuck on your estate would be very upset if you kept them waiting for a few days? Joking apart, baron, can't you postpone your trip for a few days?"

"Frankly, I can't think of anything that would induce me to do that."

"Don't be impatient with me straight away," the engineer said, raising his head and looking me in the face, "and permit me to be perfectly frank with you. I was at the Racing Club last night and talked about you with some good friends of yours, in fact you were the subject of a pretty lively discussion. No, you're not the man I first took you for, you're not an intellectual or an aesthete. Whenever your name was mentioned, it was in a strange tone of respectful hatred. It was said that in some of your affairs you displayed a certain – shall we call it a certain broad-mindedness in your choice of means. Someone referred to you as a splendid rogue – please remain seated, I am reporting facts, I have no intention of offending you. You want to go to your estate to shoot roebuck. I understand. But why? You're not responsible for Eugen Bischoff's death, you can't be. After all, if only half of what I was told about you was true, I don't understand why in this instance you did not defend yourself, why you did not give my friend Felix as good as you got from him."

"And I, sir, don't understand what all this – what Felix has to do with my going away for a few days' shooting."

"Do you want to play hide-and-seek with me?" asked the engineer, looking at me seriously. "Why? Don't deceive yourself, none of your friends will fail to remark on your talent for skilful stage management, even if in the newspaper accounts of your hunting accident there is no specific reference to it."

I had to think for a few seconds before I realised what he meant. I rose to my feet, for I had no desire to continue this conversation. The engineer rose too. I realised from the flickering of his eyes, his flushed cheeks, and the fidgety movements of his hands that the alcohol was beginning to have its effect.

"It's always disagreeable to meddle in other people's affairs," he went on in a kind of excitement. "All the same, I suggest to you that you postpone your trip for two days. I appreciate that you are in a situation in which you have no choice. But if I promise you that Felix and I will tell you the name of Eugen Bischoff's murderer within forty-eight hours?"

This made no impression on me, I did not take it seriously, I was convinced that it was merely the alcohol that made him talk with such arrogant self-assurance. I felt challenged by this, and had an abrupt refusal ready on my lips. But then it occurred to me that he might have come across some new fact, some detail that had eluded me the day before. I don't know how it happened, but suddenly I felt practically certain that he knew something that I did not, and it seemed to me to be perfectly conceivable that he might have discovered a clue of some sort in the pavilion enabling him to draw conclusions about the identity of the unknown stranger whom he called the murderer.

"Fingerprints?" I asked.

He looked at me uncomprehendingly and did not answer.

"Did the murderer leave fingerprints in the pavilion?" I asked.

He shook his head.

"No, there were no fingerprints or anything of that kind. Listen. The murderer has never been in the villa. Eugen Bischoff was alone in the pavilion the whole time."

"But yesterday you said . . ."

"That was a mistake. No-one was with him. When he fired the two shots he was wholly under the influence of an alien will – that's my view of the situation today. The murderer was not with him either at the time or beforehand, because I know he has not left his home for years . . ."

"Who?" I exclaimed in surprise.

"The murderer."

"You know who he is?"

"No, I don't. But I have reason to believe he's an Italian who knows hardly a word of German and, as I said, has not left his flat for years."

"And how do you know that?"

"He's a monster," the engineer went on, ignoring my question. "A kind of monster, a man of huge physique, obviously morbidly fat and consequently condemned to complete immobility. So much for his physique. And the strange thing about it is that this repulsive creature has an extraordinary attraction for artists. One was a painter and the other an actor, hasn't that struck you?"

"But how do you know that physically the man's a monster?"

"A monster. A human freak of nature," the engineer repeated. "How do I know that? You now think me a marvel of perspicacity, but actually I only had a bit of luck in my inquiries."

He interrupted himself and looked attentively at the wood carving of the armchair in front of my desk.

"Biedermeier chairs are known for their fragility, aren't they?" he said. "This furniture certainly isn't Biedermeier. Is it Chippendale? Well, Dr Löwenfeld overheard a telephone conversation in the director's office that Eugen Bischoff had with a lady who may have been the one to whom you spoke yesterday. Do you know Dr Löwenfeld?"

"The director's secretary?"

"Dramatic adviser or secretary or producer, I don't know what his job at the theatre is. I met him this morning and he told me . . . Wait a moment."

The engineer produced a tram ticket from his waistcoat pocket on the back of which he had scribbled some notes.

"Dr Löwenfeld remembered the conversation word for

word," he went on. "This is what Eugen Bischoff said: 'You want me to bring him? Impossible, my dear lady. Your Biedermeier furniture would never stand the weight – and there's no lift where he lives, how could I get him down the stairs?' That was all. Then came some of the conventional phrases with which one ends a telephone conversation."

He carefully folded the ticket and looked at me inquiringly.

"Well?" he said. "What do you think of that?"

"I think it rather hazardous to draw such far-reaching conclusions from those few words," I said. "How do you know it was the murderer whom they were talking about?"

"Who else could it have been?" the engineer replied. "The man who can't go out because there's no lift in the building he lives in is the murderer, I'm certain of that. I now know what he's like. A freak of pathological bulk, and very likely lame into the bargain. Do you think it will be very difficult to find him?"

He began developing his plans for my benefit, striding up and down the room.

"For one thing, there's the Medical Association whom we could ask. A 'case' of that kind could hardly be unknown to the specialists. Then there's the fact that human beings of that size nearly always have heart trouble. So I may be able to find out more about him from a heart specialist. He's an Italian, and apparently doesn't understand a word of German, and that further reduces the number of possible suspects. But I hope to be able to save myself the trouble of following up all these possible leads, because I think there will be a much simpler way of finding the murderer. There's only one thing I don't understand. What attracted Eugen Bischoff to this Italian? Did he have a taste for monsters and freaks of nature?"

"How do you know the murderer is an Italian?" I asked.

"To say I know it would be an over-statement," the engineer replied. "It's only a conclusion I've drawn. No doubt you'll again call it hazardous. That doesn't matter. I'll try to explain to you why I'm convinced that the murderer must be Italian, and then you can say what you like about it."

76

He collapsed into the armchair and rested his chin on the backs of his clasped hands.

"I must go back to the prehistory of the case," he began. "Do you remember that the naval officer whom Eugen Bischoff told us about set out to track down his brother's killer? We know what happened. One day he came home unusually late for his midday meal, and he committed suicide an hour later. That day he had found and spoken to his brother's murderer. That's clear to you, isn't it?"

"Yes."

"Then listen to this. In the last days of his life Eugen Bischoff similarly came home very late, the first time on Wednesday and the second time on Friday. He came by taxi, because at table he mentioned that he had some trouble ahead with the police – his driver had collided with the trailer of a tram in the Burggasse, and he would have to give evidence. On Saturday, when he came home late again, he was tired, distracted and monosyllabic. Dina assumed that rehearsals had gone on longer than usual, but did not ask about it. Today I discovered that on all three days rehearsals ended at the usual time. So you see that in both cases the circumstances that preceded the crime were the same. I can see only one difference, but it's an important one. You know what I'm referring to?"

"No."

"Strange that it hasn't occurred to you. Well, the murderer exercised a strong suggestive influence over his victim. To all appearances the naval officer succumbed to this on the very first day. In Eugen Bischoff's case it took the murderer three days to impose his will. Can you explain that to me? Actors in general are easily suggestible people, one would expect a naval officer to put up a much more energetic resistance. I have thought about it, and have found only one satisfactory explanation. The murderer speaks a language familiar to the naval officer in which, however, Eugen Bischoff could make himself understood only in clumsy and roundabout ways. From that I conclude that the man must be an Italian, for Italian was the only foreign language of which Eugen Bischoff had any knowledge. You may be right, baron, it's a hypothesis and a very bold one, that I admit . . ."

"It could be you're right," I said, for I remembered that Eugen Bischoff really was a great lover of Italy and all things Italian. "Your train of thought strikes me as completely logical. You have almost persuaded me."

The engineer smiled. An expression of satisfaction appeared on his face. My admission obviously gave him pleasure.

"I admit that I should have hit on those ideas myself. All honour to your detective acumen. I no longer doubt that you'll discover the identity of the lady to whom I talked on the telephone yesterday before I do."

The smile vanished from his face and furrows appeared on his brow.

"Not much detective acumen will be needed for that, I'm afraid," he said slowly. He raised his hands and dropped them again, and that gesture betrayed a resignation the reason for which I did not understand.

He relapsed into silence. He took a cigarette from his silver cigarette case and held it between his fingers. He was so lost in thought that he forgot to light it.

"You see, baron," he said after a pause, "while I was sitting here waiting for you, I had – it won't be easy to make the association intelligible to you – well, while I was sitting here I was naturally thinking about the lady on the telephone and her really strange reference to the Day of Judgment – I myself don't know how it happened – but suddenly I saw the five hundred dead of the Munho river."

He stared blankly at the cigarette in his hand.

"That is, I didn't see them," he went on. "But something made me think what it would be like if I were confronted with five hundred yellow distorted faces, all of them desperate at the certainty of death, looking at me accusingly . . ."

He tried to strike a match, but it broke.

"A childish idea, of course. You're right," he said after a while. "What does that shadowy phrase mean to people of the present day? The Day of Judgment, an empty phrase from the past. God's Judgment Seat. Do those words rouse any feeling in you? Of course when the sound of the *Dies Irae* resounded from the pulpit your forefathers were stricken with mad terror and went down on their knees. The Yosches" – he suddenly assumed a casual, conversational tone as if what he was talking about, while perhaps not uninteresting, was not of any real importance – "the Yosches come from a very Catholic area, the Neuburg Palatinate, don't they? I see you're surprised that I know so much about your family background. Don't imagine that I normally take any interest in the genealogy of baronial houses, but one likes to know with whom one is dealing, so last night at the club I looked up the Almanach de Gotha . . . What was I saying? No, I wasn't frightened, no, of course I wasn't, that would have been absurd. All the same, it was a very strange feeling. Brandy is an excellent way of getting rid of troublesome ideas."

His cigarette was alight at last, and he leaned back and blew blue smoke rings into the air, I watched them, and all sorts of ideas came into my head. Suddenly I felt I had found the key to the engineer's strange character. This fair, broad-shouldered giant, this robust and determined man of action, had his heel of Achilles. He had talked about this long-past war experience for the second time in twenty-four hours. He was no drinker, to him drink was merely a sanctuary, a place of brief refuge from a desperate struggle in which he was involved. A burning sense of guilt that would not heal over followed him through the years and gave him no respite. The slightest reminder of it cast him down utterly.

The clock on the mantelpiece struck eleven. The engineer rose to say goodbye.

"I have your word for it, haven't I? You're postponing your trip," he said, and held out his hand.

"What gave you that idea?" I said irritably, for I had not given him any such assurance. "I have not changed my plans. I'm leaving today."

"Is that so?" he exclaimed angrily. "Have I been wasting

my time? I've spent two hours trying to get you to see reason, and . . ."

I looked him in the face. He immediately saw that this was not the way to talk to me.

"I beg your pardon," he said. "I've been very stupid. At bottom the whole affair is no concern of mine."

I accompanied him out. He turned in the doorway and struck his brow with his hand.

"Of course," he exclaimed. "I nearly forgot the most important thing. Listen, baron. I saw Dina this morning. I may be mistaken, but I had the impression that she would very much like to talk to you."

This piece of information was like a blow on the head with a rifle butt. For a moment I stood there in a trance, totally unable to think. For the next second I had a wild struggle with myself. I wanted to go to her, take her by both shoulders – he had been with her, seen her, spoken to her. I felt a wild desire to find out everything, good and bad, to ask him whether she had mentioned my name, and if so what the expression on her face had been. That was my first impulse, but I overcame it. I stayed quite calm, I did not give myself away.

"I'll let her know my address," I said, and noticed that my voice was trembling.

"Do that. Do that," the engineer said, and slapped my back in very friendly fashion. "Have a good trip. And don't miss your train."

TWELVE

I do not find it at all easy to explain why I did not carry out my intention to leave by the next train. It was certainly not the thought of Dina that kept me in Vienna because, however much I was struck by what the engineer told me, after a moment's calm reflection I attached no importance to it. She believed me to be her husband's murderer. Was it really possible that she wanted to see me again? I saw through the engineer's purpose. He had invented the story to dissuade me from leaving Vienna, and I was furious with myself for having been taken in by it; if only for a second.

The reasons that made me give up the idea of going away were by no means of a compelling nature, they resulted from a change of mood brought about by the engineer's visit. Hitherto I had been quite inactive. An absurd incident had put me at the centre of an event to which I did not feel I had the slightest connection. I had been so stunned by the sudden turn of events that I had hardly tried to defend myself. I had completely withdrawn into myself, left everything to the chance that was governing events and, in an inexplicable reversal of feeling, had wanted only to remain unaffected by memories of the events of the previous day.

That had now changed. The conversation with the engineer had roused in me the desire to take up my own cause myself. Eugen Bischoff's murderer must be found, and I did not know where to look for him. I imagined a dreadful, sluggish, monstrously fat creature craftily waiting for his victim between his four walls. The idea that this murderous horror was more than a figment of the engineer's imagination, that he might be living in my immediate neighbourhood, that I might confront him and call him to account – it was this last thought in particular that spurred me to action. I had wasted far too much time already, now I mustn't waste another minute. I must find out where Eugen Bischoff had been between twelve and one o'clock on three days of the past week, that was the point from which everything else would follow, and I set about the task with the impatient zeal that had prompted me to make preparations for leaving town during the night.

By now it was one o'clock. Vinzenz had laid the table, but I left untouched the meal that he fetched as usual from a neighbouring tavern when I was at home. I paced up and down the room in a state of nervous excitement, made plans, dismissed them as useless or impractical or too time-consuming, considered all sorts of possibilities, but obstacles kept cropping up, I embroiled myself in a hundred different schemes, lost patience and began all over again, and not for a single moment did I doubt that I would end by hitting on the right one.

Inspiration came suddenly, when I least expected it. I was standing by the open window. The activity in the street reflected in the windowpanes was strangely diminished in size, and the picture it presented is inscribed in my memory as with an etching tool. I can still plainly visualise the bluish white curtains in the windows opposite, the lady with the old-fashioned cloche hat who was crossing the road, the working-class woman carrying a basket full of lemons. I could make out distinctly, though on a miniature scale, the Archangel Michael raising his hands in a protective gesture on the counter of the chemist's opposite. A passing tram obscured the picture and released it again. A confectioner's van was standing outside the corner café, and a red-haired apprentice carrying two yellow-brown boxes disappeared through the revolving door. And while I watched all this an idea struck me that seemed so simple and obvious that I could not understand how the engineer had managed not to think of it.

The starting point of my investigations must be Eugen

Bischoff's taxi accident in the Burggasse. The Burggasse was in the 7th district, I reflected. I knew the police superintendent there, Dr Franz or Friedrich Hufnagl. I had gone to see him a few months previously about an anonymous threatening letter that had been sent me. Since then I had come across him several times in the chess room of a café in the town; he would help me. I lacked the inner peace and patience necessary to carry out inquiries myself. I wrote a few lines on a visiting card, and called my man Vinzenz.

"Go to the police station in the Kreindlgasse, ask for Dr Hufnagl, and give him this card," I said. "He will let you look up the police report of a road accident. Note the driver's name and the number of his cab. Then you will wait for the driver at his rank and bring him here, I've got to talk to him. That's all. Have you understood? You'll find that the police will be helpful."

He went off, leaving me plenty of time to consider my chances, which I certainly did not overrate. Very likely I would find out where Eugen Bischoff had picked up that taxi. That wouldn't get me very far, but at least I would know in what part of the city I must begin my search, and it was clear to me that it was then that my real difficulties would begin. But I counted on luck or sudden inspiration to help me out when the time came. Also I had stolen a march over the engineer, and that was good enough for the time being.

I had to wait for two hours, and the time passed very slowly. Vinzenz came back at three o'clock with a copy of the police report, from which it appeared that according to Police Constable Josef Nedved, taxicab no. A VI 138, driver Johann Wiederhofer, at 1.45 on 24 September because of the slippery road surface had skidded into the trailer of city tram no. 5139 in the Burggasse and suffered slight damage. The driver, whom Vinzenz had found at his rank, was waiting with his vehicle at the front door.

Johann Wiederhofer turned out to be a very loquacious gentleman of mature years. He obviously had not yet got over the accident, which had brought him into contact with the

83

police, and he violently objected to any kind of police interference and to the tendencies to solidarity that in his opinion characterised all tramwaymen.

The mishap had been due to no fault of his, he insisted. It had been raining, and it had rained on the previous day too. The collision had occurred suddenly and out of the blue, and only his vehicle had been damaged. But those rogues the tram drivers all backed one another, and all at once the policeman had appeared on the scene, and he had told him not to make a fuss or take any notice of those tramway types.

He lit a Virginia cigarette, and I took advantage of the pause to ask about the extent of the damage. A mudguard had been bent and scratched, the windscreen had been smashed, and he had lost a whole afternoon doing repairs, which he finished on Saturday morning. At midday he was back at his rank, and chance had it that the same gentleman came out of no. 8. "Don't you take him," his colleagues had said, but he wasn't superstitious, not he. "Get in, sir," he had said to the gentleman, and . . .

"You saw the gentleman from no. 8 coming?" I interrupted, unable to conceal my excitement. "Where is your rank?"

"On the Dominikanerbastei, just opposite the Popular Café," he replied.

"Take me there," I said. "Dominikanerbastei 8," I said and got into the cab.

It stopped outside a melancholy-looking three-storey building. I looked in vain for the porter's flat inside the dark doorway, and found myself in a very neglected courtyard – puddles of rainwater had formed on the stone paving. A dog of indeterminate breed standing on a hand-cart barked at me furiously. Two pale small boys on a rubbish heap were playing with box lids and broken tiles and bottles. I asked one of them where I could find the caretaker, but he did not understand and did not answer.

I stood there for a while, at a loss what to do. A continual splashing sound came from some corner or other, perhaps from a fountain, or water may have been overflowing from the eaves. The dog was still barking. I went up the winding wooden staircase, intending to knock at a door and ask for information.

I was met by an unpleasant smell, the smell of domestic refuse, accumulated damp, and decaying vegetable matter. I was unwilling to give up and leave empty-handed, so I overcame my distaste and forced myself to go on.

On the first floor I did some reconnoitring. The premises of the Hilaritas German Students Association were on the right, next to the staircase. Two letters were under the door and a crumpled note on which "Am at the Kronstein café" was scrawled in pencil, followed by an illegible signature. There seemed to be no point in seeking information there, and the same applied to the office of the Hat and Felt Goods Dealers' Association. The third door was that of a private flat, occupied, according to the nameplate, by Wilhelm Kubicek, Major (ret.). I rang the bell, and handed my card to the girl who opened the door.

She showed me into a simply-furnished room. White covers protected the furniture. Opposite the door there was a portrait of a lieutenant field marshal in full dress uniform with the Order of the Iron Crown on his chest. The major, in dressing gown and slippers, came towards me, and on his face I read surprise and uneasiness at a visit the purpose of which he could not explain. On the table were a magnifying glass, a hookah, a note-pad, a cleaning rag, a bar of chocolate and an open stamp album.

I explained that I had called in order to seek information about a fellow-tenant of his. I had felt justified in seeking aid from an ex-officer, for I was a captain (retired) in the 12th Dragoons. The mistrust vanished from his face. He asked a trifle uncertainly whether I had called on behalf of some business and, when I told him that it was a purely private affair that had led me to him, his reserve disappeared. He regretted he could not offer me a glass of schnapps, a good Kontuczowka he had from Galicia, but his wife had gone out and taken the key with her. He couldn't even offer me a cigarette, as he was a pipe-smoker.

I described the man I was looking for exactly as the engineer had described him to me. The major was surprised to hear that the building in which he lived harboured anyone of such extraordinary physique. He had never heard of the monster.

"Strange, strange, strange," he muttered. "I've lived here ever since I left the army. The whole street is a gossip shop and, if Frau Dolezal from no. 6 has ox tongue with caper sauce for lunch, every child in the street knows it the same afternoon. You say he never goes out? But one would have heard something about him, no-one could have remained so completely hidden as that. Do you know what I think, captain? Someone has been taking you in. If you will forgive me for suggesting such a thing, captain, I think some humorist has been pulling your leg."

He stopped and thought for a while.

"On the other hand," he went on, "didn't you say he's an Italian? Just a minute, just a minute, just a minute. Until last year a Serbo-Croat lived in this house, his German was very bad, I was the only one who could talk to him in his mother tongue because for two years I was stationed at Priepolje, a kind of sin-bin, you know, it gives me the creeps to think of it, the stories I could tell you about Novibazar, but never mind about that now. He wasn't really fat, quite the reverse in fact. His name was Dulibic, I now remember, and he was the nephew of a parliamentary deputy, they're all traitors, if you ask me, and if I had my way – but you can't mean him, because he moved to Budapest last year. Dulibic his name was, that's right, Dulibic. But just a minute, just a minute. There is someone I haven't seen for two or three weeks. What has happened to Herr Kratky? I asked the caretaker's wife, one never sees him any more. He had inflammation of the middle ear. He's going out again now, he's still rather pale and weak, it takes time to get over a thing like that. But for one thing he's not an Italian, and for another he's not really what one would call fat."

He thought again for a while, and suddenly he seemed to have an idea.

"Supposing the man you want is Herr Albachary, after all," he said, lowering his voice, and he smiled cautiously and understandingly. "There's really no need for you to feel any embarrassment with me, why should you, we're both old soldiers, after all, and I myself was young once. Herr Gabriel Albachary lives at no. 8 on the second floor. You've no idea of the people who go up and see him, many of them are men of breeding and proper gentlemen, after all anyone can find himself in a situation in which he needs Herr Albachary, I think nothing of it. Also he's said to be a highly educated man, a great connoisseur and collector in the face of the Lord, pictures, antiques, theatrical relics and relics of old Vienna, all sorts of things, he's an old gentleman, always elegant, always smartly dressed, the only thing is that he takes ten, twelve or fifteen per cent, all depending, and sometimes more."

I had no desire to be considered a moneylender's client, so I decided to take the major into my confidence so far as the circumstances required.

"I am not in financial difficulties, major," I told him firmly, "and I am not interested in Herr Albachary. To put it in a nutshell, I am here because of the actor Eugen Bischoff, of whom you have heard, perhaps, major. In the past few days he was here a number of times, and by all appearances there is a connection between those visits and his suicide. Last night he shot himself at his villa."

The major leapt from his chair as if he had had an electric shock.

"What did you say? Bischoff, the court actor?"

"Yes, I very much want to find out . . ."

"Killed himself? Impossible. Is it in the papers?"

"It's bound to be."

"The court actor Bischoff? Why didn't you tell me straight away? Of course he was here. The day before yesterday, no, wait a minute, about twelve o'clock on Friday . . ."

"Did you see him, major?"

87

"No, but my daughter did. The things you say! The actor Eugen Bischoff. What do the papers say? Money troubles? Debts?"

I did not answer.

"It must have been nerves," he went on. "An artist nowadays, over-worked and over-strained – that's what my daughter thought too – he looked distracted and distraught, he didn't realise at first what she wanted of him – yes, these brilliant people – my daughter – we both have our hobbies. I collect jubilee stamps and special issues. When I've completed a collection, I sell it, one can always find an enthusiast willing to buy. My daughter's more interested in autographs. She has a whole album full of them. Painters, musicians, excellencies, actors, singers, all sorts of celebrities. At midday on Friday she came dashing in. 'Whom do you think I ran into on the stairs, papa?' she said excitedly. 'Eugen Bischoff, just imagine it.' She picked up her album and dashed out again. An hour later she came back looking radiant, she had had to wait all that time on the stairs, but she got him, and he wrote his name in her book."

"And where had he been all that time?" I asked.

"At Herr Albachary's, where else would he have been?"

"Is that just an assumption, or . . . ?"

"No, she saw him come out. Herr Albachary accompanied him to the door."

I rose and thanked the major for his information.

"Do you want to go already?" he said. "If you've got a moment to spare, you might be interested in my collection. I've no great rarities, only what comes my way."

And he pointed with the stem of his pipe to the open album and said:

"Honduras. The latest issue."

A few minutes later I was at the door of Herr Albachary's flat and rang the bell.

A red-haired youth as long as a bean pole and in his shirt-sleeves opened the door and let me in.

88

No, the gentleman was not at home. When would he be back? That was impossible to say. Perhaps not till the evening.

I could not make up my mind whether or not to wait. From the half-open door of the room I heard footsteps and the sound of someone impatiently clearing his throat.

"That's another gentleman waiting to see Herr Albachary," the young man explained. "He has been waiting for half-an-hour."

My eyes fell on the clothes rack, where a raglan and green velour hat were hanging, and a black polished walking stick with an ivory handle was leaning against the wall. Good heavens, I said to myself, I know that hat and coat and stick. Someone I know is here. The idea of being greeted in a moneylender's waiting room by an acquaintance was the last straw. I must clear out fast, before he had the idea of looking to see who the new arrival was.

I said I would come back another time, perhaps next day at the same time, and hurried out.

Down in the entrance hall I suddenly remembered where I knew that hat and coat and ivory-handled stick from. So great was my astonishment that I stopped in my tracks. It was incredible. How could he have found his way here before me? But there was no doubt about it. The man whose overcoat was upstairs in the waiting room was the engineer.

THIRTEEN

It was raining in torrents when I walked out of the entrance hall. The street was practically deserted, and the driver, wrapped in a mackintosh, was sitting at the wheel reading a dripping newspaper. I felt uneasy. I could not see how the engineer had managed so quickly and so certainly to follow Eugen Bischoff's invisible trail but, to tell the truth, I quickly gave up worrying about it. All I knew was that my sleuthing had been totally superfluous. The inquiries at the police station, my questions to the driver, my call on the old major had been a useless waste of energy. It had been a wasted afternoon. I felt hungry and tired, I was shivering with cold, and the rain blew in my face. All I wanted was a dry change of clothing and a warm room. I must get home as quickly as possible.

The driver, who had been having some sort of trouble with the petrol tank, stood erect. "Myrthengasse 18," I called out to him – that was my address. But just when we were moving off I had an idea that completely changed my mood. I had been thinking that the trail I had been following had led me up a blind alley, but that was not the case, it led further. That accident had happened in the Burggasse. Strange that it struck me only now, but the Burggasse was not on Eugen Bischoff's way home. Why had he gone so far out of his way?

I told the driver to stop, and I started questioning him in streaming rain in the middle of the road.

"Where was the gentleman going on Friday when you had that accident with the tram?"

"To the Myrthengasse," he replied.

This annoyed me.

"Why don't you listen?" I exclaimed angrily. "Didn't you hear what I said? The Myrthengasse is where I want to go now, Myrthengasse 18. What I asked you was where that gentleman was going on Friday."

"He was going to the Myrthengasse," the driver calmly replied.

"What? To no. 18, where I live?" I exclaimed in surprise.

"No, sir, not to you, to the chemist's."

"What chemist's? The Archangel Michael's?"

"I only saw one chemist's shop in the street, it may be called that, sir."

What could be the meaning of this, I wondered as we drove on. He goes straight from the moneylender's flat to a chemist's, and to one that was not on his way home. That was strange, but there must have been a reason for it. There was no doubt in my mind that there was a connection of some sort between Eugen Bischoff's visit to the moneylender and his taxi ride to the chemist's. What a triumph it would be if I discovered what it was. I assured myself that perhaps this would not be so very difficult, I had been intending in any case to buy some bromine, and I would simply go to the chemist's and there would be no difficulty in striking up a conversation. Confidentiality? Pharmacists were under no obligation of confidentiality – or perhaps they were. Never mind, I would have to go about it tactfully, I'd ask the elderly chief pharmacist, who always cringed to me so abjectly – your humble servant, baron, I hope to have the honour again soon – or the proprietor himself, or . . .

I had been racking my brains all day, and now, by this chance – but of course it wasn't chance that had led Eugen Bischoff to the Archangel Michael's Pharmacy, he had gone there for her sake, he had known her from her childhood and entrusted himself to her. And I had seen her every day from the windows of my flat hurrying to lectures at the university with her briefcase full of books, small, fair-haired with a reddish tinge, always in a hurry and always excitable, and not long ago I had seen her in the vestibule at the theatre – that was why her voice on the telephone had struck me as so familiar, and now I realised why it had reminded me of an unusual odour, ether and turpentine, of course, the pharmacy smell.

I was beside myself with excitement, for I realised the importance of my discovery. I couldn't help thinking of the engineer wasting his time sitting and waiting in the old moneylender's flat – while I – in two minutes I would be with the girl who had used that strange phrase the Day of Judgment, the obscure meaning of which was somehow connected with Eugen Bischoff's suicide. The moment when the answer to the tragic riddle would be revealed seemed imminent, and I looked forward to it with vague apprehension and uneasiness, and at the same time with impatience and hope.

Her name was Leopoldine Teichmann, and she was the daughter of a great actress who had died young, a woman of unforgettable beauty whose name was never mentioned without passionate admiration in the world in which I grew up. The girl had inherited from her mother her reddish fair hair and a certain restless way of life, and perhaps also a burning ambition, for she had dabbled in many arts. She painted. I remembered an oil painting she once exhibited, a still life of long-stalked asters and dahlias – incidentally a very mediocre work. She made many appearances as a dancer in performances for charity, and she once surprised Eugen Bischoff with a proposal to take drama lessons from him, but this never got beyond the stage of preliminary discussions. Some time after this she disappeared from the circles in which she had played a certain role. Faced with the necessity of earning a living, she had qualified as a pharmacist and, as I had completely lost her from sight, I was very surprised when one day she turned up as an M. Pharm. at the Archangel Michael's chemist's shop.

It was still raining when I reached the Myrthengasse. I stopped in front of the chemist's window and, while contemplating through the rain-dimmed windows the display of liniment bottles, tubes of toothpaste and powder boxes, I thought about the best way of opening the conversation. I ended by deciding to introduce myself to the girl as a friend of Eugen Bischoff's and asking whether I might talk to her alone.

The chief pharmacist grovelled almost as soon as I opened the door. "My respects, baron," he said, "please step this way, I'm at your service, what can I do for you?"

The shop was full of customers. A bank clerk was trying to find a prescription in his wallet, two housemaids were waiting to be served, a pale young man in horn-rimmed spectacles was reading an illustrated weekly while waiting, a barefooted small boy wanted ribwort sweets, and an old lady with a shopping bag wanted eye drops, marshmallow tea, Prague ointment, and "something to clear my blood". The proprietor was sitting at his desk in a neighbouring room. Fräulein Teichmann was nowhere to be seen.

"What dreadful weather," the chief pharmacist complained, pouring spirit of soap into a bottle. "I expect you've caught a cold, baron. I always recommend a glass of mulled wine, preferably with a stick of cinnamon, and nutmeg and cloves, well sweetened, goes down very nicely. Then inhalations at night – that will be eighty heller, Herr von Stiberny, it's an honour, sir, thank you very much, good-bye, Herr von Stiberny, always at your service."

He pointed to the pale young man with horn-rimmed spectacles as he left the shop, waited for a moment, and then turned to me and said *sotto voce*:

"That gentleman who has just gone out – he's a very interesting case, he's a haemophiliac, commonly known as a bleeder. He has been to all the doctors and professors and specialists, but they can't help him. A bleeder, there's only one in a thousand."

"Herr Stiberny? Oh dear, that's news to me," said the old woman with the shopping bag.

I asked for some sleeping pills, and was given a number of small white tablets in a little cardboard box.

"Isn't the young lady who generally serves me here today?" I asked.

"Fräulein Poldi?"

"The young lady with reddish fair hair, yes, I think that's her name."

"This was her morning off, as she was on night duty yesterday. She should turn up at any moment, she should have been here an hour ago. Can I give her a message?"

"It's not necessary, I'll drop in again later," I said. "It's not important, I just wanted to pass on greetings from a mutual friend whom I met in Graz. I was passing and just looked in. You might give me her address."

I could see from the chief pharmacist's face that he was not convinced by my story of a mutual friend in Graz. He looked at me searchingly, but wrote down her address on a piece of paper, and said as he handed it to me:

"No. 21 on the second floor, at Court Councillor Karasek's, that's the young lady's grandfather. She comes from a very good family, and she's said to be engaged, at any rate that's what I've been told."

Leopoldine Teichmann's address, according to the note that the chief pharmacist gave me, was Bräuhausgasse 11. As she might have been on her way to the chemist's and I did not want to miss her, I did not go there straight away.

I walked up and down outside the chemist's shop and waited. About six o'clock another heavy downpour made me go up to my flat, where I could keep the chemist's shop door under observation from my bedroom window.

The time passed and she did not appear. It began to get dark, and I could only with difficulty make out the faces of the people who came and went. When I heard the first shutters being lowered in the street down below I left my observation post, for it seemed unlikely that she would be coming now.

So I would have to go and find her. It would take about twenty minutes to get there, I decided, and she would be having supper, which would be inconvenient – not the time for a stranger to call, and she might not even be there, she might be at the theatre or at a girl friend's. Never mind, it couldn't be helped, I had to see her today, I'd go there and wait for her.

94

I spent a lot of time trying to pick up a taxi, and it was nearly eight o'clock when I at last arrived in the Bräuhausgasse. No. 11 was a desolate four-storey suburban block of rented flats. A cinema, a second-hand clothes shop, a hairdressing saloon and a bar occupied the ground floor. The stairs were badly lit, and the second floor was in complete darkness. I had no matches on me and tried in vain to decipher the numbers on the doors.

I heard footsteps. Two men were coming up the stairs in the dark. I stopped and listened. They reached the second storey. A pocket torch was lit, a small circle of light fell on one of the doors, glided along the wall to the right and back again, and then made a nameplate appear out of the dark.

I heard the voice of Dr Gorski, who was standing next to me.

"Friedrich Karasek, Court Councillor retired," he read aloud.

"Doctor!" I exclaimed, taken aback. "What brings you here?"

Light from the pocket lamp shone on my face.

"So you're here, baron," I heard the engineer say.

"So are you," I exclaimed in dismay, "and you don't seem in the least surprised to see me here."

"Surprised? You're joking, baron. I didn't doubt for a moment that you too read the evening papers," said the engineer and pulled the doorbell.

FOURTEEN

I did not understand what he meant by this, I was still completely taken aback by this unexpected encounter. Only when an old woman opened the door and I saw her tearful face and distraught eyes did I realise that some sort of disaster must have occurred.

The engineer introduced himself.

"My name is Solgrub," he said. "I telephoned an hour ago."

"The young Herr Karasek would like you to wait for him," the old woman whispered. "He'll be back in a quarter of an hour, he just hurried over to the hospital. Come in, gentlemen, but quietly, please, so that the court councillor won't hear, he doesn't know yet, we haven't told him."

"He doesn't know?" the doctor said in surprise.

"No. Half an hour ago he asked where she was, she always reads the newspaper to him in the evening. I told him Fräulein Poldi was still at the chemist's. Now he's sitting there holding the newspaper, and he has dropped off to sleep. So please come in, it's straight ahead, young Herr Karasek will soon be back."

"Biedermeier furniture," the engineer noticed, and exchanged a knowing look with Dr Gorski. Then he turned to the old woman again and said:

"Is young Herr Karasek the court councillor's son?"

"No, he's his grandson, he's Fräulein Poldi's cousin."

"And did it happen here, in this room?"

"No, in the small room over there, where the young lady has her laboratory. This morning I was in the kitchen talking to Marie, I'm the housekeeper, I've been here for thirty-two years, I was in the kitchen when the young gentleman came

96

in. 'Frau Sedlak,' he said, 'quick, a glass of hot milk.' 'Who wants hot milk?' I said, 'the court councillor?' 'No,' the young gentleman said, 'it's for Poldi, she's lying on the floor and she's having cramps,' and when I heard that I said: 'Cramps? You frighten the life out of me' – the young gentleman was quite calm, nothing seems to upset him, and of course I took the milk from the hearth and hurried in, and there she was, throwing herself about on the floor, and her face was as white as chalk and her lips were blue, and I said 'She's having a fit' and I grabbed her hands, and then I yelled 'Jesus, Mary and Joseph, she has a bottle in her hand,' and the young gentleman called out 'What is it, why are you shrieking like that?' and then he saw the bottle and took it and smelled it and dashed to the telephone and told the operator to put him through to the First Aid Society, and they arrived a few minutes later, it was lucky they were so quick, and the doctor from the First Aid Society said so too, he said it wasn't a minute too soon, and perhaps there might still be hope. And he said it was inconceivable that she could have made a mistake, she was a trained pharmacist, and must have recognised the smell at once. Excuse me, I must go back to the kitchen, I'm alone in the flat, and if the court councillor wakes up he'll be wanting his creamed rice."

She shut the window, adjusted the yellow silk cover on the piano, cast a critical eye at the room, decided everything was in order, and went out. I rose to look at the pictures on the wall. There were watercolours and pastel paintings, amateur work, a chestnut tree in full bloom, a portrait of a young man playing the fiddle, a not very well composed country marketplace, and also the picture I had once seen at an exhibition, asters and dahlias in a green-shimmering Japanese vase, so it had never found a buyer. But more than by all these I was attracted by a picture hanging half in shadow on the wall next to the piano. It was an oil painting of the beautiful Agathe Teichmann as Desdemona. I recognised her immediately, though it was nearly twenty years since I had seen her.

"Strange to see her again after twenty years," I said to the doctor, pointing to the picture of the great tragedienne. I was overcome with sadness, I felt how remote from me my own youth had become, for a moment I was aware with painful clarity of the passing of the years, the relentless flight of time.

"Agathe Teichmann," the doctor said, adjusting his pince-nez. "I saw her on the stage only once. Agathe Teichmann. How old were you then, baron? You must have been very young, nineteen or twenty at most, I should think. A not entirely untroubled memory, is it? I never had any luck with women, you see. On the other hand, nowadays I can look at an old picture without being at all affected. I saw her that once as Medea, that was all."

I did not answer. The engineer looked at us both uncomprehendingly, shook his head, gave the picture a fleeting glance, and went across to the small room.

We were left alone and waited. The doctor grew impatient and kept looking at his watch. The time passed slowly for me too. I picked up a book that was lying on the desk and opened it, but it was a dictionary, so I put it down immediately.

After a quarter of an hour the engineer at last came back. He seemed to have been looking for something on the floor, for his hands were dirty.

Dr Gorski sprang to his feet.

"What did you find, Solgrub?" he asked.

"Nothing."

"Really nothing?"

"Not the slightest trace. Not the slightest clue," the engineer repeated and looked absent-mindedly at his hands.

"There's water over there, Solgrub," said the doctor. "You're on a false trail, can't you see that? You've been chasing a phantom all day. Your monster doesn't exist and has never existed, he's the absurd result of false reasoning, a figment of the imagination – how many more times must I repeat that? You've got an absurd idea fixed in your head and are getting nowhere."

"And what would you do, doctor?" the engineer asked from the wash basin.

"We must try to influence Felix."

"That's hopeless."

"Give me time."

"That I can't do. Are you blind, doctor? Don't you see how he sits there saying nothing and lets us talk? He'll never agree to his word of honour being made a subject of discussion with a very uncertain outcome. He has made his decision, he'll do what Felix wants him to do, perhaps tomorrow, perhaps tonight, his finger's on the trigger, and you ask for time."

I wanted to answer, to protest, but the engineer prevented me.

"I'm on the wrong track, of course," he exclaimed. "That's what you told me this morning, doctor, at the taxi rank outside the theatre when I asked for the driver who took Eugen Bischoff to his murderer. Then, when I had found the house and went up the stairs you called out after me that I was on the wrong track, I had a fixed idea in my head . . ."

"You were at the moneylender's flat?" I interrupted.

"The moneylender's? What moneylender are you talking about?" the engineer said in surprise.

"Gabriel Albachary, Dominikanerbastei 8."

"Is he a moneylender? You never told me that, doctor."

"He lends money on security, that is true," said the doctor. "He's not an acquaintance to be particularly proud of. On the other hand, he's one of our most important connoisseurs and art collectors. Eugen Bischoff knew him for nearly twenty years, and sometimes used his Shakespeare library and his collection of pictures of costumes."

"Did you talk to him?" I asked the engineer.

"No, he was out, and I used the opportunity to search the flat for the murderer."

"And with a result we'd prefer not to talk about, eh Solgrub?" the doctor pointed out.

"Keep quiet," the engineer exclaimed loudly, and immediately lowered his voice, remembering he was in someone else's flat. "It's true I haven't found him, but only because I painted a false picture of him in my mind, that's why I haven't found him. There's a false link somewhere in my chain of argument. But the killer's up in his flat and can't leave it, doctor, and I'll find him, you can be sure of that."

And as he said that it roused something in me, it was a kind of pride, and it made me want to deprive him of his certainty, to lead him astray, to plunge him into doubt.

"And supposing I tell you that Felix is right?" I said cold-bloodedly and with full awareness of what I was doing. "Suppose I tell you that what happened was exactly as he described it yesterday? Supposing I confessed that I really am Eugen Bischoff's murderer?"

Dr Gorski grabbed my arm and looked at me dumbfounded, and the engineer shook his head.

"Nonsense," he said. "Don't talk nonsense. You don't imagine you can lead me astray, do you? Listen, there's the bell. It's young Karasek. Please let me talk to him."

FIFTEEN

"He thinks we're reporters," Dr Gorski whispered to me. "Let him. That's what Solgrub wants. It's just as well you're in civilian clothes. A captain of dragoons in uniform claiming to be a representative of a local newspaper would have been . . ."

The young man who came into the room at that moment created the impression of being one of those extremely insignificant persons who preside and play the part of *arbiter elegantiarum* at suburban cafés. "My name is Karasek. This is an honour, gentlemen," he said. He drew his hand across his carefully flattened hair and offered us cigarettes from his alpaca cigarette case.

"It's very kind of you to have found time for us after the events of a day such as this," the engineer said. "First of all may I ask you how the young lady is?"

"Certainly, certainly," young Karasek replied. "I am fully aware of the duties and responsibilities of the press – never off duty, night or day. My late father had a great deal to do with you gentlemen, he was Hermann Karasek, chairman of the 18th district, municipal architect, one of you gentlemen may perhaps have . . . yes, my cousin, unfortunately they wouldn't let me see her."

He bent forward and said in a low voice, as if he were betraying an official secret:

"The professor is now trying ethyl chloride."

"Inhalations, presumably," Dr Gorski remarked.

"Ethyl chloride," the young man repeated. "They are leaving nothing untried."

"Did you talk to the doctor?" the engineer asked. "Do you

think it's possible that the young lady may be well enough to see visitors tomorrow morning?"

"Tomorrow morning? Hardly, hardly," the young man said, shaking his head. "The doctor thinks – the professor, as you can imagine, was very busy and didn't have time, but I talked to his assistant – he said one must never give up hope, but unless there's a miracle, and the sister also said that probably she won't survive the night."

"Is it as bad as that?" said the engineer.

Young Karasek regretfully raised his hands and dropped them again. Dr Gorski rose and picked up his hat.

"Are you leaving already, gentlemen?" the young man said. "Won't you stay a few more minutes? I know that for you gentlemen it's after dinner, but a cup of black coffee, it won't take two minutes, I'll order it straight away. I also wanted to ask which of you gentlemen it was with whom I had the honour of talking on the telephone, I should be interested to hear."

"It was I who called you," said the engineer.

"How was it that you knew? That perplexed me, as they say. Yes, she was a heavy smoker, twelve or fifteen cigarettes a day, she often had a cigarette in her mouth before breakfast – girls nowadays – it happens. My grandfather mustn't be told, he's an old gentleman, an octogenarian, a gentleman of the old school. But how did you know that immediately beforehand – less than five minutes before . . . I was amazed. How did you know that?"

"The explanation is very simple," the engineer replied. "Your cousin's attempted suicide was not voluntary but enforced, as I can tell you. There have recently been three quite similar cases of enforced suicide, the last of them barely twenty-four hours ago. In all these cases the same person was involved, and in all three cases the method was the same. So immediately beforehand the young lady asked you for a cigarette?"

"No, she did not ask me for a cigarette. She had a whole boxful on her desk. What she asked for was a cigarette paper."

"A cigarette paper?" the engineer exclaimed excitedly. "Of course, I should have thought of that. Do you now see why Eugen Bischoff took that pipe? One more question before we go, Herr Karasek, and perhaps you will think it a strange one. Did your cousin recently mention the Day of Judgment? Do you understand what I said? The Day of Judgment."

"Yes, Herr . . . What did you say your name was?"

"Solgrub, Waldemar Solgrub," the engineer replied impatiently. "And in what connection did she mention it? Think, and perhaps you'll remember."

"In what connection? In connection with painting. That was her idea when she was with Ladstätter and me a few days ago – but first I must explain that Poldi is engaged to an office-friend of mine, a very decent fellow who comes and sees her every day, they wanted to get married in the spring. They don't have a great deal of money, but he has a good job, and she has a profession and earns too – she has a trousseau and the furniture and everything is ready, and grandfather has given his blessing. Well, on Thursday last week a small party of us, a few girls and a few men colleagues, had supper at the Stag, one of the men was celebrating his name day, and on the way home – the three of us, Poldi, Ladstätter and I, went on ahead, Ladstätter had his guitar with him, and suddenly Poldi once more started talking about how unhappy she was at the chemist's and how much she wanted to go back to painting and, instead of letting her talk, Ladstätter stopped and started squabbling with her. 'Poldi,' he said, 'if you're serious, you must know what you are doing, but if you don't mind about our getting married in March – you know I don't have much money and that I'll have to count on what you earn too, at any rate at first, and if you give up your job at the chemist's . . .' 'And who says I won't earn far, far more from painting?' Poldi answered, and Ladstätter said: 'You've had two exhibitions and haven't sold a single picture. It's no good banging one's head against a brick wall, and unless one has connections . . .' and Poldi said quite calmly that this time she was going to be successful. 'Why should you be?' Ladstätter

103

asked, and Poldi answered calmly that this time she was going to do much better work. She could rely on the Master of the Day of Judgment for that."

"The Master of the Day of Judgment?" the engineer interrupted. "Who in heaven's name is that? Do you know him?"

"No, I don't, and Ladstätter too wanted to know who the devil he was. 'Another painter who asks you to his studio?' he said, and Poldi laughed and said: 'Are you jealous, Ludwig? You have no need to be, really you don't. If I told you how old he is . . .' But Ladstätter flushed scarlet. 'Whether he's old or young, Poldi, I want to know who he is, and I have a right to know,' and Poldi looked at him and said: 'Yes, Ludwig, you have a right to know, and when I'm famous I'll tell you. I'll tell you, Ludwig, and nobody else. But only when I'm famous and not before,' and by that time the others had caught up with us, and nothing else was to be got out of her the whole evening."

"Doctor," the engineer said, "we now know all about his methods, don't we? We know the trap and we know the bait. The only remaining puzzle is the motive. What does he gain by his mischief? But please go on, Herr Karasek. What happened next?"

"At midday next day Poldi came home with a strange gentleman, and that reminded me of the whole thing. A tall, well-built gentleman, smoothly shaven, no longer very young and already greying slightly, and Poldi went past me straight to her room without introducing me, which is not Poldi's usual behaviour, and I said to myself that Ladstätter certainly wouldn't like Poldi being alone with that strange gentleman, on the other hand I didn't want to be intrusive, I decided it would be better to wait till the gentleman left and then stop him and ask him straight out what he wanted of Poldi. But when I looked into the room half an hour later the gentleman had gone. The book was lying on the table, and I pointed out to Poldi that the gentleman had forgotten it, it was a fat dictionary that was worth something, after all . . ."

"He left a book here?" the engineer interrupted. "Where is it? Can I see it?"

"Certainly, there it is," the young man said, and the engineer picked it up from the desk. It was the book I had idly leafed through half an hour before. He looked at it, and let out a cry of surprise.

"It's Italian," he exclaimed. "An Italian dictionary. So who was right, doctor? The monster speaks Italian, that proves it. Eugen Bischoff had it with him to make himself intelligible to the monster. But what's that? Look, doctor, what does that mean?"

Dr Gorski bent over the book.

"Vitolo-Mangold. Encyclopaedic Dictionary of the Italian Language," he read from the title page. "Rather too compendious. Difficult to handle. A real reference book," he said.

"Doesn't anything else strike you?"

Dr Gorski shook his head.

"Really? Are you sure?" said the engineer. "Then look at it more carefully. Herr Karasek, you saw the gentleman coming. Are you sure he didn't have another book with him?"

"He only had that one. I'm sure of it."

"That's very remarkable. Look, doctor, it's an Italian-German dictionary. There's no German-Italian section. To all appearances Eugen Bischoff didn't need the German-Italian section. What's the explanation of that? Eugen Bischoff didn't talk to the killer, but listened to him in silence. Just a moment, don't disturb me. One talks and the other remains silent and listens and translates. What's the meaning of that? Let me think."

Suddenly I heard a high, tremulous, old man's voice from the door. "Frau Sedlak is sitting and weeping in the kitchen. What has happened to Leopoldine?"

Court Councillor Karasek, Agathe Teichmann's father, whose noble Goethe's head remained vividly in my memory from the past, had greatly changed. An old, old man of spectral thinness, the very personification of frailty, was standing in the doorway, leaning on his stick and staring at the floor. His face was completely expressionless.

Young Karasek had jumped to his feet.

"Grandfather," he stammered, "nothing has happened, what do you think could have happened? Poldi's asleep on the sofa, as you can see, the poor girl has been on night duty."

"I'm worried about her," the old man sighed. "She has a mind of her own and she won't listen to me or anyone else. She has that from her mother, you know, Heinrich, from Agathe. First there was all that trouble about the divorce, and then there was more because of that rogue of a lieutenant. I came home, smelled gas, it was pitch-dark in the flat. 'Agathe' I called out . . ."

"Grandfather," young Karasek said imploringly, and on his generally so vacuous face there was now a touching expression of affectionate concern, "don't go on with that, heaven knows how long ago it all happened."

"I've got it," the engineer suddenly exclaimed quite loudly, as if he were alone in the room. "Doctor, we can go, there's no more for us to do here."

The old man raised his head.

"Have you got company, Heinrich?" he asked.

"A few colleagues from the office, grandfather."

"That's good, Heinrich, a little distraction, a little entertainment's always a good thing. A game of cards? I ask your pardon, gentlemen, for not having greeted you. My eyes are still not right. I've always been short-sighted, they told me it would get better with age. That's the opposite of what happened to me. But what has happened to Poldi, where is she? I've been sitting and waiting for her to read the paper to me."

"Grandfather," said young Karasek with a bewildered and despairing glance at us. "She's tired, let her sleep, don't wake her. I'll read the paper to you this evening."

SIXTEEN

Dr Gorski was in a foul mood. As he groped his way down the steep staircase in the dark he grumbled and swore.

"Where the devil is Solgrub?" he wanted to know. "He has my pocket torch, and he goes ahead and leaves me in the lurch. What sort of manners is that? Careful, more stairs. Baron, where are you? Go on ahead, I've lost my way. Do I turn right or left? If at least I had some matches, but I haven't. I know you can see in the dark, I've always said there was something cat-like about you. That silent bow of yours upstairs was priceless, what did you think you were doing? Didn't you realise that the old man's blind? Completely blind. Heaven forbid that I should ever get as old as that. Light at last. Hallelujah, the Lord be praised, we're down at last."

A thin mist lay over the street, the sky was overcast, the gas lamps threw feeble gleams of light on the wet pavement. People were waiting for admission to the cinema, someone opened the door of the wine bar, and for a moment I heard hoarse voices singing and the doleful music of an orchestrion.

The engineer came towards us.

"Where have you been all this time?" he said. "I've been waiting for you for ages. It's ten past nine, too late to go and see the Spanish Jew today."

"Gabriel Albachary?" said the doctor. "Why on earth do you want to see him again so soon?"

"Why do I want to see him? Doctor, you're slow in the up-take, a schoolboy would be quicker than you. I want to see the Master of the Day of Judgment again. This afternoon . . .

107

Why are you looking at me like that? The monster. Don't you realise what I mean? Eugen Bischoff's murderer."

Dr Gorski shook his head.

"You think the old man was the killer?"

"What old man?"

"The Spanish Jew."

"God in heaven, doctor, you have an infernal capacity for confusing things. Listen to this. First of all, there's the cigarette paper. It's not difficult to see the part it played. Then there's the book, the dictionary. I opened it and saw that it was the key to the problem. That made it necessary to think, to concentrate, but then the old man, the court councillor, appeared and started asking questions – I didn't listen to him. Systematic thinking, doctor, is no mere empty illusion. The murderer didn't listen, he only spoke – what did that mean? Now I know. It's all in order now. That's nothing to brag about, the whole day has been full of mistakes. He really is a monster, a colossus, and I sat facing him for an hour without realising it."

We were walking slowly down the street. Dr Gorski nudged me. "Did you understand?" he said.

"Not a single word," I replied.

The engineer looked at me crossly.

"There's no need for you to understand," he said. "Why should you, what for? Everything's in order, be satisfied with that. You can sleep peacefully tonight. You won't be going away. There won't be any shooting accident. There'll be no cross against your name in the Almanach de Gotha, at any rate for the time being – you follow me so far, don't you?"

"Won't you stop being semi-intelligible and tell us precisely what you have found out?" Dr Gorski asked.

"Not tonight, doctor. I've only a vague idea of what happened. A very vague idea, and besides – there are still gaps in the logical sequence of events. I still don't know for whom Eugen Bischoff's first shot was meant, and as long as I don't know that . . ."

"Will it ever be possible to find out?"

"It may be, doctor. What prevents me from repeating Eugen Bischoff's experiment? I may be able to give you information as early as tomorrow that should be useful to you too, baron. That's all I can tell you tonight. Be patient with me."

"If you're being serious, Solgrub – and you seem to know what you're saying – if it's an experiment you have in mind, for heaven's sake be careful, take good care of yourself."

"All right, doctor," the engineer said calmly. "Do you think I walk blindly into danger? I know exactly what I'm up against. Look . . ."

He took from his pocket a small revolver of foreign make.

"This is a good friend of mine from the old days, it was my companion on many a night patrol in the hilly country between Kirin and Gensan, but now it's no use to me, and we must part. Take it, doctor, I shall want it back. The monster up there in the Spanish Jew's flat – you know he doesn't kill, he enforces suicide: so long as I am unarmed he has no power over me."

"And what do you propose to do with him, Solgrub?"

"He must be destroyed," the engineer said quietly and grimly. "Into the fire with him. The poor girl whose life the doctors are fighting for tonight must be his last victim."

"Into the fire with him, you said? Into the fire? Then if I've understood you correctly the monster . . ."

"Ha!" the engineer exclaimed. "Doctor, I think you're beginning to understand. You've taken your time. No, he's not a human being of flesh and blood. He died long ago, but he still lives and insinuates himself into people's minds. And I'm going to put an end to the spectre. But that's enough, you'll see for yourself."

We had at last reached a livelier neighbourhood in a part of the city in which I knew my way about. We were in a wide street, brightly lit by arc lamps, with acacia trees on either side of the roadway. The barracks of the 23rd Regiment cannot have been far away.

"Where have you led us?" Dr Gorski complained. "We've

made a quite unnecessary detour, I could have been home long ago."

"I've no intention of letting you go home yet," said the engineer. "That's the Gulliver Café over there. Won't you take an Allasch with me?"

Dr Gorski declined the offer for both of us without consulting me.

"I'm going home by tram," he announced. "Yes, by tram," he continued with a glance at me. "I'm not an officer, and have no status to live up to. You two can stand and wait here till a taxi turns up."

"Oh, nonsense, come in with us," the engineer said. "If you're lucky you'll meet an interesting man. My friend Pfisterer is a regular here, he's a true polymath, a man with a Barnum circus memory, a historian as well as a dancer, a painter, an engraver, actor, barman, Jack of all trades, paragon – and he's an expert in keeping his creditors at bay, though there are at least five hundred of them."

"Thank you, but I don't like long-haired geniuses," the doctor said grumpily.

"My friend Pfisterer is of the porcupine variety, besides being just the man I need today. Come on, I've no desire to go home alone tonight."

We went into the café. It was a rather dubious sort of place, and our arrival made a definite impression on the few customers. The engineer seemed to be well known here, as the young woman at the pay-desk greeted him with friendly condescension.

A reluctant waiter approached and asked for our orders.

"Is Dr Pfisterer still here?" the engineer asked him.

"Hasn't been anywhere else all day," said the waiter with a gesture implying contempt and well-justified mistrust.

"How much does he owe here?"

"Twenty-seven kronen, not counting tips."

"Here are twenty-seven kronen plus a tip," the engineer said. "Where is Dr Pfisterer?"

"He's over there in the billiard room as usual, busy writing."

A tall, thin, red-haired man was sitting at one of the marble tables with a half-empty beer bottle, an egg cup he was using as an ink pot, and a pile of handwritten pages in front of him. A quite young girl with hair dyed bright yellow was sitting silently by his side, making cigarettes. A dirty sheet of paper, fixed with a drawing-pin to the wall facing him, was covered with closely written pencilled handwriting. On closer inspection this turned out to be a document of far-reaching significance. It was as follows. "Announcement. The undersigned regretfully withdraw the charge of theft against Dr Pfisterer of stealing two illustrated weeklies and an illustrated supplement as he has threatened to take proceedings against us. (Signed) The table of the four."

"There he is," said the engineer. "Good evening, Pfisterer."

"Good evening. Don't disturb me," the red-haired individual replied without looking up.

"What are you working on, may I ask?"

"The thesis of a young idiot who badly wants a doctorate. Waiter, some stewed pears with a disgusting amount of syrup, and a Turkish coffee à la Pfisterer. I've got to finish this by eleven o'clock."

"Let me have a look. May I?" the engineer said, and picked up one of the handwritten sheets. "Pectins and glycosides as vegetable-flavouring substances," he read. "Since when have you been a chemistry expert, for heaven's sake?"

"I know as much about it as the members of the faculty at the university," the great scholar replied, and went on with his writing.

"Can you spare a moment, Pfisterer? I need some information."

"If you must, but make it snappy. The boy's coming at eleven o'clock to fetch his life's work."

"Is there a painter known to the history of art as the Master of the Day of Judgment?"

"Giovansimone Chigi, a well-known master, a pupil of Piero di Cosimo. Next question."

"Lived when?"

"1520, in Florence, you ignoramus."

"Did he commit suicide?"

"No. He died mentally deranged in the monastery of the Seraphic Brothers of the Seven Dolours."

The polymath put down his pen and looked up. He had a glass eye and on his right cheek a red birth-mark.

"Is that all you want to know?"

"Thank you, yes."

"Your thank you doesn't get me very far. You put three questions to me, as Mime did to Wotan, the Father of All. Now it's my turn, and I'm putting three questions to you, Solgrub. No. 1. How are you off for cash?"

"I've paid your bill."

"Splendid. I don't know that I've any other questions to put to you. Solgrub, go your way. I've long since noticed that you've disgracefully gone over to the moneyed section of humanity. Disgusting. Get out of my sight."

We drank our Allasch standing.

"Mentally deranged," the engineer muttered. "He has stronger weapons than I suspected. Mentally deranged? Nonsense. I fought in the east and I'm not afraid of his Last Judgment."

SEVENTEEN

A strange idea struck me at breakfast next morning. I tried to drive it away by thinking of more serious and important matters, but it would not leave me in peace and kept coming back, so I ended by giving in to it. I rose, took five of the white tablets the chemist had given me, and dissolved them in a glass of water. My eyes fell on the packed suitcases that were still in the room, for I had been intending to go away. Now I would have to abandon the project, for that absurd and crazy idea of mine had put it out of court.

However, when I sat down at my desk, the idea no longer seemed quite so stupid and ridiculous. Sleeping dreamlessly from one night to the next, cheating the devil of a grey autumn day, breaking the tyranny of the hours by an easy movement of the hand – something inside me murmured: Why wait? Do it now.

I picked up the glass and held it in my hand. No, not yet, I told myself, I've got to go out. There were some important matters to be attended to, things that I could not postpone. Later on, I muttered to myself, perhaps this evening, and I put the glass back on the desk.

When I came back at midday I found a note from the engineer on the desk.

"I have some important news for you," it said. "I appeal to you urgently not to go away or do anything until I've spoken to you. I'll be with you this afternoon."

I had not intended to go out again in any case, so I stayed at home. I took a book from the book case and settled down at my desk.

At about five o'clock a storm broke – thunder, lightning, a real cloudburst. If I hadn't shut the windows quickly the room would have been flooded. Then I stayed by the window and watched people scurrying for shelter. The street was swept clean of human beings in a moment – that amused me. Then the bell rang. There he is, I said to myself, he would turn up in a storm like this.

Important news. Well, we'll see. I did not hurry. I put the book I had been reading back in its place, picked up a sheet of paper from the floor, and put the armchair in front of the desk back where it belonged. Then I walked out of the room.

"Vinzenz, where's the gentleman who asked for me?" I called out. No-one had asked for me. The afternoon post had brought me the long-awaited letter from Jolanthe, the young lady of the Stavanger fjord. A big white envelope with no seal and no trace of perfume – that was just like her. I had called her Jolanthe in jest, after the heroine of some French novel the title of which I had forgotten. The name had not met with her approval, however, it was not her style, her name was Auguste. Well, she had written at last, this was the letter she had promised. That's good, I said to myself, now it's my turn to write. She kept me waiting long enough, now she can wait a bit, I said to myself, and put the letter unopened into a pigeon-hole in the desk.

At seven o'clock I gave up waiting. By that time it was dark, rain was still pattering on the windowpanes and black clouds hung over the roofs. He won't be coming any more, it's too late, I said to myself. Won't this rain ever stop? The glass into which I had dropped the white tablets was still there. No, not yet, it's not the right time yet. First I must put my papers in order. I had kept putting off that troublesome job, but it had to be done. Documents, notices, maps, crumpled or folded letters, ballast accumulated over the years – I could hardly find my way about the jumble in the desk. I told Vinzenz to make a fire in the grate, the room grew warm and comfortable, and I took a pile of dusty paper from the bottom drawer – and by some strange chance on the top of the pile were my exercise books from the military academy. I looked through one of them, and was struck by the clumsy writing of a sixteen-year-old. *The Territorial Reserve acts in support of the armed forces as a whole. Universal conscription. This must be served in person – substitution is not permitted. Krakow, Vienna, Graz, Budapest, Pozsony. Nine Territorial Reserve and six Honved territorial districts. Mother's birthday Wednesday* hastily written in the margin. *Mountain artillery. Portable recoil-operated quick-firing gun with removable shield, baggage train, took vehicle, eight mules for transport of rations. Tuesday the 16th, route march, fall in four a.m.* The dawn of my life, that's how it all began. Away with the rubbish, into the fire with it.

Letters from my guardian, who died half a life-time ago. Photograph of a girl I could not remember, with a date, 24 February 1902, written on the back, and with the words: Let it be true friendship that brings us together. The diary of a girl who died young, begun on 1 January 1901 at Dr Demeter's sanatorium, Merano. A big sketch done with coloured pencils. Details of the sale of 1200 cubic metres of beech and oak wood sent me by my estate manager. A catalogue in my own handwriting of my collection of Javanese and Annamite pictures on cloth, together with a letter of thanks from the Natural History Museum, anthropology department, for presenting the collection to them. A map of the Rottenmanner Tauern. An engraved invitation to a court ball. Letters and more letters, and a more recent photo given me when I said goodbye to the daughter of the Dutch consul in Rangoon at the bottom of which she had written something in Singhalese characters. "You'll never find out what I wrote, so don't try," she told me, and as I looked at the photo now I still didn't know whether the curly writing meant love or hate. Into the flames with it all. The picture from Rangoon wouldn't catch fire at first, but the heat was too great, and fire consumed the proud eyes, the slightly furrowed brow, the slender figure and the undeciphered message.

"I'm sorry, I'm very late," a voice said suddenly from the door. "Are you alone, baron? Isn't Solgrub here yet?"

I jumped to my feet. I must have failed to hear the doorbell. I was dazzled by the glow of the fire, and in the semi-darkness I could not make out who this caller was. "I knocked, but there was no answer," this late visitor said, and closed the door behind him. "Hasn't Solgrub been here?"

He took a pace nearer, light from the table lamp fell on his face, and at last I recognised him. He was Felix, Dina's brother. What on earth could have brought him here?

"Solgrub? No, I haven't seen him since yesterday," I said.

"Then he'll be here soon," Felix said, and took the seat I offered him.

"Solgrub, my old friend Solgrub, has an *idée fixe*. He believes you to be totally uninvolved in the events that led to Eugen Bischoff's death, and he asked me to be here so that he could tell me the results of his inquiries in your presence."

I listened in silence and said nothing.

"We two know what really happened, baron," Felix went on. "My old friend Solgrub is a fantastical fellow, and has a slight tendency to make a fool of himself. He connects the suicide of a young lady who is completely unknown to me with that of my brother-in-law, and he talks about an experiment from which he expects to draw important conclusions, and he insists on the influence of a mysterious stranger – heaven knows I didn't find it easy to listen quietly to him. If I have understood him correctly, his system of erroneous deductions is based on the fact that Eugen Bischoff fired two shots, one at an unknown target and the other at himself. If Solgrub does as I expect, that is, if he confesses his error to us, I will tell him the answer to the riddle of the first shot. Eugen Bischoff had never used his revolver, so he fired a trial shot before turning the weapon against himself. That's the obvious explanation. Strange that Solgrub isn't here yet."

"Do you want to wait for him?" I asked abruptly, because I wanted to put an end to this conversation.

"If I'm not disturbing you."

"Then allow me to continue with what I was doing."

I did not wait for an answer, but took a packet of letters from the desk and began to look through them.

"That green Bosnian prayer mat," said Felix, his eyes wandering through the semi-darkness of the room. "How long ago was it that I last sat here facing it? I was a volunteer in your regiment, and I came here to ask your advice in a matter that was very close to my heart. *Eheu fugaces* . . . That time you talked to me like a friend, baron . . . Is everything going into the fire, baron?"

"Yes, everything. Rubbish from the past. The engineer won't be coming any more tonight. It's nine o'clock."

"He certainly will be coming."

"In the meantime can I offer you something? Sherry? A cup of tea?"

"No, thank you. But may I ask you for the glass of water that's on the desk?"

"I don't advise you to drink that," I said, and rang for Vinzenz. "Those are the sleeping pills I prepared for tonight."

"For tonight," Felix repeated quietly, with a long, piercing look at me.

A few minutes passed. Vinzenz came in, I gave him the order, and he went out noiselessly. I continued dealing with those old papers.

"I was wrong not to ask you up this morning," Felix said suddenly. "When I looked out of the window again half an hour later you had gone. Perhaps you had the entirely intelligible wish . . ."

I interrupted, not with a word or a gesture, but with a look of surprise.

"I saw you in the garden in front of the villa, walking up and down in the rain – or was I mistaken?" he went on, slightly disconcerted.

"What time was that?"

"Ten o'clock."

"That's hardly possible," I replied calmly. "At ten o'clock I was at my lawyer's. I was with him from nine to nearly eleven."

"Then I was deceived by a quite extraordinary resemblance."

"Presumably," I said and felt anger mounting inside me. He was still convinced he had seen me standing outside the villa windows hoping to catch a glimpse of Dina, I could read that in his eyes. I could contain myself no longer, a wild desire overcame me, a desire to hurt him, to wound him in his pride. I felt for the picture, which I found at once, the picture I had never shown anyone. For a second I held it in my hand, I held it in a way that he could not fail to see it, I saw him grow pale and the hand in which he was holding a glass of water trembled – and then with a casual gesture I threw it into the fire.

Cramp seized me, I felt a stab near my heart, the memory of a winter night flashed through my mind, I wanted to grab the picture back from the flames with my bare hands, but I controlled myself and watched it burn to ashes. All was dark in front of my eyes, all I could see was the glow in the fireplace and the white-bandaged hand and nothing else.

I heard Felix's voice. "Now I have the answer for which I came here," he said. "To tell the truth, I was not sure what your intentions were and I used the night to prepare for all eventualities by committing to paper the matter that concerns us both. Now, of course – I have understood you, baron. You have made your decision, and it's final. Otherwise you would not have parted with that picture."

He produced a big white envelope from his breast pocket and held it so that I could see to whom it was addressed.

"This is the letter," he said. "It has become unnecessary. Permit me to use the opportunity that has presented itself."

He threw the letter, which was addressed to the commanding officer of my regiment, into the fire.

At that moment I realised that the time had come and that my fate was sealed and, as this certainty dawned on me, the day that was just drawing to a close underwent a strange transformation in my mind. It seemed to me that from early morning the only idea in my head had been that I must die because I had betrayed my word of honour, and everything I had been busy with that day now revealed to me its secret meaning. It had not been a mere mood that made me destroy my papers – I had done it because I wanted to die – I must leave nothing behind in this world of unremitting, prying curiosity. I had left unopened the long awaited letter from Norway, the letter from Jolanthe – whatever it contained, there was no point in opening it. And there the glass was waiting for me, the glass that meant sleep, sleep with no awakening.

"The bell rang," Felix said. "That's Solgrub. Let him come and spin his fairy tales. He won't change your decision."

I heard footsteps, Solgrub, the engineer was coming, I feared the moment when he would walk in, whatever he was going to say would sound crazy, ridiculous, absurd. I saw the derision on Felix's lips.

"Come along, Solgrub, come in," he called out. "Come in and tell us your news."

Not the engineer, but Dr Gorski appeared in the doorway.

"So it's you, doctor," Felix said. "Are you looking for Solgrub?"

"No, I was looking for you. I was at your place, and they sent me here."

"Who sent you here?"

"Dina. I haven't told her. I told her nothing. Solgrub . . ."

"What about Solgrub?"

Dr Gorski took a step forward, stopped and gazed at me.

"Solgrub – at seven o'clock, I was still holding my surgery when the telephone rang. 'Who's speaking?' – 'Doctor, for heaven's sake, doctor.' 'Who is it?' I asked, I didn't recognise the voice – 'Doctor, for heaven's sake, tell Felix . . .' – 'Solgrub!' I exclaimed, 'is that you? What has happened?' – 'Get back,' he yelled in a voice that was no longer human, 'Get back.' After that I heard nothing except what sounded like a chair being upset. I rang again, but there was no answer. I dashed down, took a taxi, dashed upstairs, no-one opened the door – I dashed down again like a maniac and fetched a locksmith – he opened it with a skeleton key – Solgrub was lying flat on the floor, with the receiver in his hand . . ."

"Suicide?" Felix asked, with a dazed look in his eyes.

"No, heart failure. It was the experiment," Dr Gorski said. "There's no doubt that he was the victim of his experiment."

"And what was it he wanted to tell me in his last moments?"

"He wanted to tell you the name of his murderer, Eugen Bischoff's murderer."

"His murderer? Didn't you say it was heart failure?"

"The murderer has many weapons, and that is one of them. I know where to find him. We must make him innocuous. Solgrub is dead, and now it's up to us. Do you hear, Felix? And you, baron . . ."

"Please don't count on me," I replied, "I'm engaged all day tomorrow."

Felix turned towards me, and our eyes met.

"No," he said. "Not now."

He took the glass that was on the desk and emptied the contents on the floor.

EIGHTEEN

On the morning after Solgrub's funeral we met in the front garden of a small café near the city park away from the main thoroughfares. It was a bright, rather frosty day. Street traders came to our table and offered us pears, grapes, blackthorn branches and winter cherries, and a Bosnian had knives and walking sticks for sale. The proprietor's tame jackdaw hopped about looking for crumbs. Felix had asked for newspapers, but did not look at them, and we sat there gazing across at the park and exchanging monosyllabic remarks about the time of year, holiday plans, and Dr Gorski's unpunctuality.

At last, at about nine o'clock he appeared. He apologised. He came straight from the hospital, where he had done the night round, and he had performed an operation at seven a.m. He drank a cup of hot black coffee standing at the counter.

"That's my breakfast," he said. "That, followed by a cigar. Sheer poison for the nerves. My only advice to you is not to follow my example."

Then we set off.

"Swedes, cabbage, pickled herring, cheap cigarettes," Dr Gorski remarked as we climbed the stairs to the Albachary flat. "This is just the right atmosphere for the task ahead. We're humble people, baron, and it's only natural that you should need a loan. Not a big one, let us say two or three thousand kronen, and you've brought your sureties with you. The man's certainly mistrustful, we mustn't startle him. One more flight of stairs. Let us hope he's in, otherwise we shall have to wait."

Herr Gabriel Albachary was in. The red-haired manservant showed us into a drawing room cluttered with *objets d'art* of all styles and periods. Herr Albachary appeared almost immediately. He was a short gentleman of exaggerated, almost dandified elegance, with moustache dyed a deep black, a monocle and a heliotrope perfume discernible from a distance of ten paces.

"Balkan," Dr Gorski whispered to me.

Herr Albachary invited us with a gesture to sit down, and looked at us searchingly for a moment, before turning to me.

"I think I am correct, baron," he said, "in believing that you were my son's superior officer. Edmund Albachary, a one-year volunteer. Also I know your name from the turf, baron."

"Edmund Albachary, one-year volunteer," I said, vainly searching my memory. "Edmund Albachary, of course. It must have been some time ago. How is the young man?"

"How is he? Who knows? Perhaps he is well. He has not been living with me for the past year, unfortunately."

"Is he away? Is he abroad?"

"He's away, yes, he's abroad. Much farther than abroad, I'm afraid. If I travelled day and night for ten years I would not reach him. I also knew your father, blessed be his memory, baron, it must have been thirty years ago. To what can I attribute the honour of this visit?"

I felt rather embarrassed. I had not intended to mention my name. Nevertheless I decided to play the part that had been allotted me and told him what I wanted.

Herr Albachary listened politely and attentively without changing his expression, and once or twice he nodded as if in agreement with what I said.

"You have been misinformed, baron," he said when I had finished, "I'm an art dealer, though nowadays I'm only a collector. I have never been in the finance business, though occasionally I arrange loans to oblige good friends who apply to me, and I should of course gladly put myself at your disposal, baron. May I ask what sum you have in mind?"

"I need two thousand kronen," I said, and I noticed that Dr Gorski was shifting uneasily on his chair.

The old gentleman looked at me in surprise.

"I understand, baron, you have been speaking in jest. You are in urgent need of two thousand kronen, and two minutes later you offer me half a million for my Gainsborough."

I did not know what to say to this. Dr Gorski bit his lip and looked at me furiously. Felix came to the rescue.

"You are perfectly right, Herr Albachary, it was a joke," he said. "We knew you do not like showing your art treasures to every Tom, Dick and Harry, and we did not choose a very clever way of introducing ourselves to you. Is that your Gainsborough?"

He pointed to a painting on the wall facing us which I had not even noticed.

"No, that's a Romney," Herr Albachary said indulgently. "George Romney, born at Dalton, Lancashire, portrait of Miss Evelyn Lockwood. The original was in my possession, I sold it to an Englishman only a few days ago."

"So it's a copy?"

"Yes, an excellent job, not quite complete, as you see, some details are just sketched in. A brilliant young painter, recommended to me by a professor at the Academy. Too brilliant, unfortunately. He committed suicide."

"Suicide? Here, in your flat?"

"No, at home, in his own flat."

"But he worked here with you," said Dr Gorski, who intervened at this point. "In which room? Can I see?"

"In my library," the art dealer replied in surprise. "It's the best place, it has the morning sun."

"One more question, please, Herr Albachary. How long has your son been in an institution for nervous diseases?"

"Eleven months," the old man stammered, looking at the doctor with a horrified expression. "Why do you ask?"

"I have good reason to do so, Herr Albachary, as you will see in a moment. May I ask you to take us to your library?"

Gabriel Albachary led the way in silence. Dr Gorski stopped in the library doorway.

"There is the monster," he said, pointing to a huge book,

of a size such as I had never seen before, on a carved Gothic lectern in the bow window. "That is the monster. That book is responsible for the disaster that happened to your son. That book was the cause of Eugen Bischoff's suicide. That book . . ."

"What are you saying?" Albachary exclaimed. "It's true that he read that book the last time he was here. He came to look at pictures of old costumes, but when I left he was standing in front of the lectern. 'Stay as long as you like, Eugen, I'm going to have lunch,' I told him, we were old friends, I had known him for twenty-five years. 'If you want anything, ring for the servant,' I said, and he said he would. That was the last time I saw him, because when I came back he had gone, and the gentleman who was here three days ago also asked to see the book, and made notes, and said he would come back."

"He didn't come back, he couldn't, he died that same evening. Where did the book come from?"

"My son brought it back from Amsterdam. What is the meaning of all this, for heaven's sake? What is in the book?"

"That we shall find out straight away," Dr Gorski said, opening the heavy, copper-lined cover. Felix stood behind him, looking over his shoulder.

"Maps," Dr Gorski exclaimed in surprise. "*Theatrum orbis terrarum*, an ancient geographical work."

"Maps engraved on copper and coloured by hand," Felix read aloud. "*Dominio Fiorentino. Ducato di Ferrara. Romagna olim Flaminia*. Nothing but maps. Doctor, we've made a mistake."

"Go on turning the pages, Felix. *Patrimonio di San Pietro et Sabina. Regno di Napoli. Legionis Regnum et Asturiarum principatus*. Next come the Spanish provinces . . . Stop. Don't you see? The back is covered with writing."

"Quite right, doctor, it's Italian."

"Yes, old Italian. *Nel nome di Dominedio vivo, giusto e sempiterno ed al di Lui honore. Relazione di Pompeo del Bene, organista e cittadino della città di Firenze* . . . This is it, Felix, we have it. Herr Albachary, will you let me have the book?"

"Take it, take it away from here, I never want to see it again."

"Yes, but how, for heaven's sake? How can I take it away, I can hardly lift it."

"I'll send two strong men from my laboratory," said Felix. "It will be at my place at three o'clock this afternoon."

NINETEEN

In the name of the living, eternal and righteous Lord
of heaven and in His praise. Description by Pompeo
del Bene, organist and citizen of the city of Florence
of the events that took place before his eyes on the
night of Simon and Jude in the year MDXXXII after
the incarnation of Christ. Written in his hand.

As I shall complete my fiftieth year tomorrow and as to all
appearances a man in this city may lose his life before his time
more easily than he believes, I shall this day, after refraining
from committing it to paper for many years, confess the truth
so that it may not be forgotten and relate what happened during that night to Giovansimone Chigi, known as Cattivanza,
the renowned master builder and painter known today as the
Master of the Day of Judgment. May God forgive him his sins
as I pray He will forgive mine and those of all His creatures.

When I was a boy of sixteen I chose to devote myself to the
art of painting from which I proposed to earn my livelihood,
and my father, a silk-weaver in the city of Pisa, sent me to the
workshop of Tommaso Gambarelli, with whom I worked on
many great and fine works. But on 24 May, on the eve of the
holy feast of Pentecost, on the same day as the enemy took
Monte Sansovino, the said Tommaso Gambarelli died of the
plague in the Spedale della Scala. So in the name of God I
sought out another master and went to Giovansimone Chigi,
whose workshop was next to the second-hand dealers' booths
in the old market.

This Giovansimone Chigi was a small and surly man. He

wore a blue cloth cap with ear flaps in summer and winter alike, and anyone seeing him for the first time might well have taken him for a Barbary pirate rather than a Christian and a citizen of Florence. He was so mean that he gave me less than half a loaf a week. Before I had been with him for seven weeks I had already spent five gold florins of my own.

One evening when I came home from mathematics school my master was in the workshop deep in conversation with Messer Donato Salimbeni of Siena, a physician who was in the service of the Cardinal Legate Pandolfo de' Nerli. Messer Salimbeni was a man of fine intelligence and venerable appearance, widely travelled and highly experienced in the art of preparing medicines and potions. I knew him from my time with my previous master, when his excellent remedies had given me great relief after I caught a fever from the damp air on a ride to Pisa.

When I entered Messer Salimbeni was looking at a picture of the Madonna surrounded by angels while my master was pacing up and down in front of the fire, for it was cold. When Messer Salimbeni saw me he beckoned to me to approach.

"And this one?" he asked.

"I have only him," my master replied, with a grimace. "He paints flowers and small animals in praiseworthy fashion, and that is what he is best at and, if I needed to put owls, cats, song-birds or scorpions into my pictures, he could be really helpful to me."

He sighed, and bent down to throw two oak logs on the fire. Then he went on:

"When I was young I did much fine work and enhanced the fame of this city with my art. It was I who made the bronze St Peter which you still see in front of the altar in the church of Santa Maria del Fiore. At that time more than twenty sonnets were pinned to my door, all of them praising my work and me, and I was also showered with other and greater honours. But now I am an old man, and I can no longer do good work."

And he pointed to a Christ teaching in the temple and to a

Mary Magdalene being borne up to heaven by angels, and said:

"What you see there is nothing. I am well aware of it, and you have no need to say so, for nothing is more oppressive than adverse criticism. In my youth I saw visions, and I saw God the Father and the patriarchs, I saw the Saviour, the saints, the Virgin Mary and the angels. I saw them in marvellous fashion wherever I looked, up in the clouds and here below in my workshop, I saw them with a clarity and vividness that the intellect alone could never achieve; and as I saw them so did I paint them, and there were not many artists who were my equals. But now my eyes are dim and the visionary fire has gone out."

Messer Salimbeni was leaning against the wall. I could not see him in the darkness and only heard his voice.

"Giovansimone," he said, "all human wisdom and knowledge is patchwork and less than patchwork, is smoke and shadow in the face of the Lord. Nevertheless it has been granted me when raising my thoughts to God to solve some of the mysteries with which this transient world is filled, and I can give you back what you call your power to see visions, and I can even awaken it in those who have never before possessed it, and I can do so with ease."

My master listened attentively to this, and for a short while stood deep in thought. Then he shook his head and burst out laughing.

"Messer Salimbeni," he said, "the whole town knows that you boast of many secret arts and skills, but that when it comes to putting them into practice you always have excuses ready. What you have just been telling me was certainly no more than another of your boasts. Or did you learn the art of which you spoke at the court of the Mogul or the Grand Turk?"

"The art of which I spoke," said the learned physician, "is not one of those heathenish arts, for I owe it to the goodness of God alone. It was He who showed me the way to knowledge."

"In that case," my master replied, "all I desire is to see something of that art. But let me tell you one thing, and that is, if you make a fool of me, it will be so much the worse for you."

"Today there is not much more we can do than to agree on a day when we can do the thing," Messer Salimbeni said. "But first I advise you to consider very carefully, Giovansimone, for it is a stormy sea on which you are about to launch yourself, and perhaps it would be better for you to stay in harbour."

"You are right, Messer Salimbeni," my master replied. "This is a case for caution, for everyone knows you are my enemy, though you speak to me with the respect to which I am entitled. I cannot trust you."

"It is true, Giovansimone, and there is no point in passing over in silence the fact that there is something between us," said the Cardinal Legate's physician. "You had a quarrel with Dino Salimbeni, my brother's son, and he spoke hard words to you, and you said aloud so that all those present could hear you: 'Just be patient, the day will come when this matter will be settled,' and a few days later he was found dead on the path through the fields leading to the monastery of the Servi friars, he lay there with a dagger stuck in his neck."

"He had many enemies, and I foresaw his misfortune," my master muttered.

"It was a Spanish misericordia dagger, and the smith's name was engraved on the blade," Messer Salimbeni went on. "It belonged to a man who had fled here from Toledo, and they seized him and took him before the Eight. He denied his guilt and insisted that he had lost the weapon the night before among the traders' booths in the Old Market, but they didn't believe him and he mounted the cart."

"All honour to the verdict of the Eight," said my master, "and things that have happened are over and done with."

"Things that have happened are never over and done with," said Messer Salimbeni. "And those responsible for them have to face divine justice."

"Let me just tell you this," my master replied. "I had a commission to paint St Agnes with the book and the lamb, and I was at home working on it when Messer Cino came seeking to make his peace with me, and we drank together and parted as friends. And next day when the crime was committed I lay ill in my bed, as I have witnesses to prove. And, as truly as God is in His heaven and I pray that He will be merciful to me on the Day of Judgment, so it was and not otherwise."

"Giovansimone," the physician explained, "it is not without good reason that they call you *cattivanza*, wickedness."

When my master heard himself referred to by that name by which he was known his fury knew no bounds, for that was something he could never tolerate, and his fury deprived him of reason and he took the wheel-lock musket he kept loaded in his workshop and brandished it like a maniac and yelled:

"Get out of here, you rogue, you priest's bastard, get out of here and never let me set eyes on you again."

Messer Salimbeni turned and went down the steps, but my master ran after him with the musket in his hands, and I heard him raging and cursing outside the house for a long time.

Some while later, it was on the eve of the feast of Simon and Jude, Messer Salimbeni turned up again, and he spoke and acted as if there were nothing between him and the Master.

"The day you were waiting for has come, Giovansimone," he said.

The Master looked up from his work, and when he recognised Messer Salimbeni he grew angry again.

"What are you doing here again? Didn't I throw you out?" he said.

"This time you will welcome me," the physician replied. "I am here so that we may do what we discussed, because the time has come."

"Just go away," the Master said irritably. "You said dreadful things about me, and you shall pay for them."

"To those who have done no wrong my words did not apply," Messer Salimbeni replied, and then he turned to me and said:

"Come, Pompeo, this is no time to sit idly playing the flute. Go and get me this and this."

And he gave me the names of the herbs and substances he needed for his fumigations and the quantities he needed of each. Among the herbs there were several I knew nothing about, and there were others that grow on every hedgerow. He also wanted two pints of brandy.

When I returned from the apothecary's the two were in agreement in every particular. Messer Salimbeni took the herbs and the substances from my hands and explained to the Master that this was this and that was that, and then he made everything ready for his exhalations.

When he had finished we left the workshop, and on the way down the steps the Master showed Messer Salimbeni that he had a sword and a dagger under his coat.

"Messer Salimbeni," he said, "don't think I should be afraid of you if you were the devil himself."

We went down the Via Chiara, crossed the Rifredi bridge, and passed the fulling mill on the other side of the river and the little chapel where the marble sarcophaguses are. It was a bright night and the moon was in the sky, and at last, after we had been on the way for an hour, we came to a hill on one side of which the ground fell steeply to a quarry. Nowadays there is a house there called the Villa all'Olivo, but then goats browsed there in the daytime.

Here Messer Salimbeni stopped and told me to gather brushwood and thistles and make a fire, and he turned to my master and said:

"Giovansimone, this is the place and the time has come. Once more I say unto you: Take counsel with yourself, for he who submits to such an ordeal must be of strong and confident temperament."

"All right, all right," the Master replied. "Stop beating about the bush and begin at last."

Messer Salimbeni then very ceremoniously described a circle round the fire and led the Master into the circle, and then he threw a little of his fumigatory material into the flames, and as soon as he had done that he left the circle.

A thick cloud of smoke rose out of the fire and surrounded the Master, and for a while concealed him from my sight, and when it thinned Messer Salimbeni threw more material into the flames. Then he said:

"What do you see now, Giovansimone?"

"I see the fields and the river and the towers of the city and the night sky, and nothing else," the Master replied. "Now I see a hare running across the fields and, oh, wonder of wonders, it has been tamed and saddled."

"That is indeed a remarkable sight," said Messer Salimbeni, "but I think you will see many more such tonight."

"It's not a hare but a goat," the Master exclaimed. "It's not a goat but an oriental creature the name of which I do not know, and it makes the most extraordinary jumps and leaps. Now it has vanished."

The Master began bowing as if greeting someone.

"Look!" he exclaimed. "My neighbour the goldsmith who died last year. He doesn't see me. Poor Master Castoldo, his face is covered with sores and boils."

"Giovansimone, what do you see now?" the physician asked.

"I see jagged rocks and ravines and gorges and caves, and I see a rock, coloured black and hovering in the air, which is a great and hardly credible miracle."

"That is the Valley of Jehoshaphat," Messer Salimbeni declared, "and the rock hovering in the air is God's eternal throne and, Giovansimone, know that to me that is a sign that you are destined tonight to see things so tremendous that no human being has seen them before."

"We are not alone," the Master said, and his voice dropped to a fearful whisper. "I see people singing and rejoicing, and there are many of them."

"There are not many but only a few to whom it is granted to join God's angels in singing the glory of the Day of Judgment," Messer Salimbeni said quietly.

"And now I see thousands upon thousands, an endless host, knights and councillors and richly adorned ladies, raising their arms to heaven and weeping, and there is great lamentation among them."

"They lament what has been and cannot be again," said Messer Salimbeni. "They weep because they are condemned to darkness and are deprived to all eternity of the sight of the Lord."

"There is a terrible fiery sign in the sky that glows in a colour I have never seen before," the Master cried. "Woe is me. It is no earthly colour, and my eyes cannot stand it."

"That colour is trumpet red," Messer Salimbeni called out in a voice of thunder. "That colour is trumpet red, the colour of the sunshine on the Day of Judgment."

"Whose is the voice that calls my name out of the storm wind?" the Master cried, his whole body beginning to tremble, and suddenly he began howling, howling like an animal, and the howling shattered the silence of the night and seemed as if it would never end.

"The demons of hell are coming for me, coming for me from everywhere and the air is full of them," he yelled. In his terror he tried to flee, but the invisible host caught him and he fell to the ground and struck out at the void all round him. He rose shrieking and with terribly distorted features, he started running but collapsed again, and it was such a pitiful sight that I thought I was going to die with fear.

"Help him, Messer Salimbeni," I cried in desperation, but the Cardinal Legate's physician shook his head.

"Too late," he said. "He is lost, for the visions of the night have taken possession of him."

"Have mercy on him, Messer Salimbeni, have mercy," I yelled.

The demons of hell had seized him and were dragging him away, and he fought them, screaming, and Messer Salimbeni went towards him and stood in the way at the cliff edge just above the quarry.

"Murderer without fear of Almighty God," he cried. "Stop and confess your crime."

"Mercy," the Master cried, and fell on his knees.

At that Messer Salimbeni raised his fist and struck him in the middle of his brow so that he fell to the ground as if dead.

I now know that this was an act, not of cruelty, but of mercy, and that by that blow Messer Salimbeni freed the Master from the power of his visions.

We took him back to his workshop, still unconscious, and he lay there without a sign of life until the Angelus. When he awoke he did not know whether it was night or day. He was confused, and kept talking about the demons of hell and the terrible colour of trumpet red.

Later, when the frenzy began to abate, he became completely absorbed in himself. He just sat in a corner of his workshop staring into the void, and he would talk to no-one. But at night he could be heard lamenting and singing prayers in his room, and on St Stephen's day he disappeared from the city and no-one knew where he had gone.

And it chanced that three years later on my way to Rome I stopped at the monastery of the Seraphic Brothers of the Seven Dolours, in which the hair-band and girdle of the Holy Virgin are preserved, as well as a ball of thread spun by her own hands. I went to the chapel, accompanied by the prior, to see the holy relics. A monk was standing on a trestle there, and it took me some time to recognise him as Giovansimone, my former master.

"His mind is clouded, but his compositions are truly great," the prior said. "We call him the Master of the Day of Judgment, for that is the only thing he paints over and over again. If I say to him: Master, here a Visitation and there the Healing of the Sick or the Feeding of the Ten Thousand, he gets very angry, and one has to let him go his own way."

The sun was just setting, and pink light from the windows shone on the stone paving, and on the wall I saw the divine rock hovering in the air, and the Valley of Jehoshaphat, and the chorus of the Blessed and the multiform demons of hell and the fiery furnace of the deepest pit of hell, and among the damned the Master had painted himself, and all this was painted with such verisimilitude that I shuddered with horror.

"Master Giovansimone," I called out, but he did not recognise me. He remained absorbed in prayer, painting with trembling hands an angry cherub with as much haste as if the devils of hell were still at his heels.

That is what I have to relate about the Master of the Day of Judgment, and there is not much more that I know. When I came to the monastery again a few weeks later the chapel was empty, and the monks showed me where he was buried. On the Day of Judgment may Christ, our bright morning star, lead him and all of us into the host of the blessed.

Since that night I have never again seen Messer Salimbeni, whom I call the real Master of the Day of Judgment, and he may have returned to the distant realms of the east in which he spent so many years of his life. But I have preserved in my memory the secret of his art, and I set it down here for those who believe themselves to be intrepid and sturdy minded: Take bloodwort saturated in brandy, divide into three parts, then . . .

TWENTY

"Go on, go on," Dr Gorski exclaimed.

"That's all," said Felix. "The writing suddenly breaks off. There isn't any more."

"Impossible," Dr Gorski declared. "There must be more. The most important thing is missing – let me have a look."

"See for yourself, doctor. There's nothing else but maps, the Spanish provinces. *Granata et Murcia. Utriusque Castiliae nova descriptio. Insulae Balearides et Pytiusae.* No writing on the back. *Andalusiae continens Sevillam et Cordubam.* Not the slightest trace of writing. The story's unfinished."

"But the composition of the drug. Where did Eugen Bischoff get it from? There must be the end of the story. You must have missed a page, Felix, have another look."

All three of us bent over the book. Felix slowly turned back the pages.

"There's a page missing here," Dr Gorski suddenly exclaimed. "Here, between Asturias and the Castiles. A page has been cut out."

"You're right," said Felix. "Cut out with a blunt knife."

Dr Gorski struck his forehead with his hand.

"Solgrub," he exclaimed. "It must have been Solgrub, don't you see? So that no-one would be able to try the experiment after him. He destroyed the last page, which included the composition of the drug. What now, Felix?"

"What now, doctor?"

They looked at each other, both completely at a loss.

"Let me confess," said Dr Gorski, "that I was going to try the drug on myself, with every possible precaution, of course."

"So was I," said Felix.

"No, Felix, I should never have allowed you, a medical layman – but what's the good of arguing about that now? It's all over. Not one of us three will ever find out what was the inconceivable force that drove Solgrub and Eugen Bischoff and heaven knows how many others to a mysterious death."

He closed the heavy copper-lined cover of the book.

"It will lead no-one else astray," he went on. "Solgrub, our poor Solgrub, was the last victim. The more I think about it – the physiology of the brain gives us some leads to follow, Felix. I have a theory of my own. No, I don't think it was a vision of the Day of Judgment. I prefer to assume that in every case the effect of the drug . . ."

I jumped to my feet. I had had an idea that overwhelmed me and threw me completely off balance. I was in no condition to conceal my excitement. I glanced at Felix and Dr Gorski – they took no notice of me. I walked out of the room.

I walked quickly through the garden, giving them little time to notice my disappearance. No, the secret was not lost, it lay there, waiting for me. I alone was going to be the discoverer of the truth. Just a few more paces . . .

The pavilion door was open. Everything had been left as I remembered it that evening. The revolver was on the desk, the tartan rug lay over the sofa, the upset ink pot, the broken bust of Iffland, everything had been left where it was, and my pipe was still on the table.

I picked it up. There, under a thin layer of ashes, was the drug, a dark brown mixture, the Sienese physician's fumigatory preparation, the magic concoction that had wrung from the murderer Giovansimone Chigi a confession of his guilt.

When I struck the match I felt a slight fear of the unknown that awaited me. Fear? No, it was not fear, it was the feeling with which a swimmer dives from dry land into deep water. The water will close over his head, but he will be up again a moment later. That was exactly how I felt. I felt sure of my nerves. I waited for visions of the Day of Judgment, I waited for them with indifference, almost with curiosity. I faced the spectres and bogies of a past age with the whole intellectual armoury of a man of the present day. All you will see is smoke and shadows, I said to myself, and took a first puff at my pipe.

Nothing happened. Through a haze of blue smoke I could see Beethoven's death mask on the wall, as well as some branches of a chestnut tree moving in the wind and above them a patch of sky covered with grey cloud. A big, bluish beetle of a kind unknown to me crept across the floor, but I had noticed it beforehand. I took a second puff, and a third, and for the first time I noticed the mixture's strange, sour smell. I noticed it only for a second, it disappeared very quickly. I had the uncomfortable feeling that Felix or Dr Gorski might surprise me, and I looked out of the window. But no-one was in the garden. They were still sitting and talking and presumably had not yet noticed my absence.

I remember that altogether I took five puffs at my pipe. Then I saw a hibiscus bush in the middle of the room.

I was perfectly aware that I was experiencing a sensory illusion, no doubt reliving a forgotten memory, but the vision was of such unparalleled vividness and plasticity that I involuntarily stepped closer and counted the reddish violet flowers of the hibiscus, there were eight of them so far as I could tell, and a ninth, a deep red one, opened as I looked at it.

The hibiscus bush vanished, and gave way to the deep green of an areca palm tree. Leaning against it was a Chinese wearing a silvery grey silk robe. The first thing that struck me was his atrocious ugliness, he had the face of a newborn child, but this did not alarm me, I was well aware that my imagination, highly stimulated by the drug, was reproducing something that had been imprinted on my memory in some foreign land but in some inexplicable way presented itself to me in horribly distorted form. At this stage of the experiment I was still a calm and cold-blooded observer of a very strange optical phenomenon. I could still see the table and the sofa and the outlines of the room, but they seemed shadowy and unreal, like an obscure and confused memory of something that had happened long, long ago.

This vision gave way to one of a brick wall and an open workshop that remained motionless before my eyes for some minutes and gave me a feeling of indescribable melancholy. The inside of the shop was illuminated by the light of a black-smith's fire, and I saw two men, naked to the waist and with shaved heads. This immediately gave me a vague sense of alarm that grew into intense horror.

One of the men suddenly turned, emerged from the shop and walked towards me on legs that seemed dislocated in some strange way. His head and shoulders were bent forward and his arms dangled lifelessly from his shoulders. He stopped in front of me, raised his left arm with his right hand, the fingers of his left hand sought for me, groped for me, I felt them on my wrist, I started back and shrieked, I heard myself shriek, fear of death shook me – those eyes – those lips – the face eaten away – leprosy, I yelled inside me – leprosy, leprosy – I broke down, I hid my hands – leprosy, I moaned, and then for a fraction of a second I struggled desperately to grasp the idea that all this was only dream and illusion, but the idea faded and I was left alone with my vision of terror, carried away on a tide of fear and horror.

I do not know what happened next. I had been lost, but came back to myself. The first thing I saw was a barred window high up on the wall, too high for me to reach. In the half-darkness that surrounded me I made out a table and two chairs screwed to the floor. On the narrow side of the room there was a heavy iron bed.

I was squatting on the floor. I had the feeling I had been in this room for a long time and had had harrowing experiences in it, though I could not remember what they were. I was dimly aware of a big, very red face in front of me with a round chin and small drops of sweat on its brow which gave me a feeling of violent revulsion.

I felt thirsty, and knew without seeing it that next to the bed an iron bowl full of water was chained to the wall. I was

139

overcome by an irresistible urge to smash it to pieces, but it withstood my efforts.

The door suddenly opened, light flooded in, and two men came in. One of them was tall, broad-shouldered, clean-shaven and wore horn-rimmed spectacles, and his face was familiar to me. The other was a short, thin fellow with a small grey moustache and lively eyes, and his hands were in the pockets of his caped cloak. I looked at him, but could not connect any memory with him.

"Dementia, alternating type, attacks recurring serially," the broad-shouldered man said in a foreign language of which I nevertheless understood every word. "Under treatment for four years. Former staff officer, cavalryman, hereditary defects on both sides."

I lay on the floor and kept my eyes on him.

"Argyll Robertson pupil, heightened muscle tone, increased pressure of cerebro-spinal fluid. No, leave the door open, the warder . . . Look out!"

I dragged him to the ground and got on top of him and throttled him. Then I jumped up and out, someone went for me, I threw him off and twice punched a broad red face with a round chin, ran on, heard shouts and cries and a whistle being blown, and suddenly I was out in the open.

Trees, bushes, an endless plain. I was alone, and round me there was an indescribable silence. The landscape was dead, nothing moved, not a leaf, not a blade of grass, only small white clouds moved over a blue sky.

I suddenly realised that I had been living for years in that room between the table and the iron bed, creeping on the floor, roaring like a wild beast, flinging myself at the door again and again, and now they were coming to take me back – there they were, I could see them, they surrounded me, and I felt a nameless fear of the man with a broad, red face.

"There he is," I heard him shout, and he was standing in front of me. His broad face was twisted into a grin, small, shiny drops of sweat were on his brow, and behind his back – I knew what he was hiding from me, I shrieked and wanted

140

to flee, but they came at me from all sides and there was no help anywhere.

Suddenly the revolver was in my hand. I did not know where I got it from, it was just there, and I was holding it, I felt the deathly cold metal of the barrel.

And just when I was raising the weapon to my temple, just at that moment there appeared in the sky a tremendous fiery glow that blazed and flashed in a colour I had never seen before, though I knew its name, it was called trumpet red, my eyes were dazzled by the hurricane of terrifying colour, it was trumpet red, and it was shining on the end of all things.

"Quick, his hand!" a voice close to me said, and I felt my arm getting as heavy as lead, but I freed myself and did not want to go on living.

"This won't do, let me go," the voice yelled, and then I heard a roaring and a singing, the terrible light in the sky went out, darkness descended, for a second I saw long-forgotten things as in a dream, a table, a sofa, blue wallpaper, white curtains moving in the wind, and then I saw nothing more.

TWENTY-ONE

I awoke as if from a deep sleep. For a time I lay with closed eyes without any idea of place or time. I could not remember where I had just been or what had happened to me, and I sought in vain for some clarifying idea. Then I opened my eyes. This cost me an effort. I had to cope with great sleepiness and a sense of torpor and indisposition.

Then I realised where I was. I was lying on an ottoman in the music room in the Bischoff villa. Dr Gorski was sitting beside me feeling my pulse, and Felix was standing behind him. The subdued light of the standard lamp fell on the pages of the huge book, which lay open on the table.

"How do you feel?" Dr Gorski asked. "Headache? Giddiness? Nausea? Buzzing in the ears? Does the light hurt your eyes?"

I shook my head.

"You have an enviable constitution, baron. Anyone else . . . Your heart is all right. I almost think you'll be able to go home alone."

"You were incredibly foolhardy, baron," Felix said. "How could you – didn't you know what you let yourself in for? It was pure chance that Dina was in the garden and heard you shout . . ."

"Yes, and we arrived not a moment too soon," Dr Gorski interrupted. "You were holding the revolver to your temple. I shan't conceal from you the fact that you treated me very unceremoniously. You threw me at the wall as if I were a rubber ball, and if Felix hadn't had the happy idea . . ."

"You know very well that it wasn't my idea," Felix pointed out.

"Very well, if Felix hadn't applied Dr Salimbeni's therapeutic violence. A single blow in the middle of the forehead made you give up your suicidal intentions. You must indeed have had terrifying experiences. Do you realise how close you were to the other bank, baron?"

Then the full memory of all that had happened to me at last returned. I jumped up and wanted to tell the whole story – the leper, the madhouse, the dreadful light in the sky.

"Don't talk about it now," Dr Gorski said. "You must tell me all about it later, when you're feeling better. Leprosy, the lunatic asylum, I expected something of the sort. The case is clear, and what you've been through only confirms what I suspected. I was just starting to give Felix my ideas on the subject when you came round. So listen to me, if you don't find it too tiring. It will make a great deal intelligible to you."

He drew the standard lamp closer to him. Then he sat silently in his armchair for about a minute.

"No, I don't think the concoction was an invention of the Sienese physician,' he began. "It's very ancient, and its origin is no doubt to be sought in the East. Fear and ecstasy. Have you ever taken an interest in the story of the Assassins? Today you may have held in your hands the drug, or one of the drugs, by means of which the Old Man of the Mountain controlled men's minds."

"And now it has been lost for ever," said Felix.

"That may be regrettable from the scientific point of view, but I'm very pleased it happened," Dr Gorski went on. "When Solgrub destroyed that last page, he knew what he was doing. The fumes you inhaled, baron, had the power to stimulate the part of the brain that is the seat of the imagination, and it increased the potency of your imagination out of all proportion. Ideas that flitted through your mind took concrete form and appeared before your eyes as if they were real. Do you now see why Dr Salimbeni's experiment had a special appeal to actors, sculptors and painters? They all looked to the drug for new impulses for artistic creation. They saw only the bait without appreciating the danger they were running into."

He rose, and in a sudden outburst of feeling struck the open pages of the book with his fist.

"Don't you see the diabolical nature of the trap? The seat of the imagination is also the seat of fear. That is the point. Fear and imagination are inseparably linked. The great phantasts have always been obsessed by fear and terror. Think of E.T.A. Hoffmann, Michelangelo, Brueghel, Edgar Allan Poe . . ."

"It wasn't fear," I said, and the memory made me shudder. "I know fear, I've experienced it more than once. Fear can be overcome. It wasn't fear or terror, it was a thousand times worse than that, it was a feeling for which there are no words."

"You know fear, baron? You claim that you know it? Since today perhaps you do. But your previous encounters with it were mere pale reflections of an experience that has been extinct in us for thousands of years. Fear, real fear, the fear felt by primitive man when he stepped out of the light of his fire into the dark, when lightning flashed from the clouds, when the cries of antediluvian saurians re-echoed from the swamps, the primeval fear of a hostile environment felt by lonely man – that is an experience unknown to modern man, who would be incapable of standing up to it. But the nerve capable of reviving it is not dead, it does not stir and shows no sign of life, it may perhaps have been drugged for thousands of years – but we carry about a terrifying sleeper in our brain."

"And that terrible light? That unimaginable colour?"

"Perhaps there may be a physiological explanation of that remarkable phenomenon too. But first I must tell you something about the structure of the human eye. It is the retina, or rather a system of nerve fibres ending in the retina, that is sensitive to colour and is stimulated by the basic colours, that is, by rays of quite definite wavelength. Isn't it conceivable that the poisonous fumes you inhaled brought about such an alteration in your retina that it became receptive to other rays of greater or lesser length? That puzzling trumpet red may have been the colour, invisible to us, that lies outside the solar spectrum and is known to physicists as infra-red."

"What are you saying?" said Felix. "You are talking of dark heat rays. Do you claim that he saw them, that his eye perceived them as colour?"

"He may have done," Dr Gorski replied. "The phenomenon is open to a number of different interpretations. But what is the point of making hypotheses that can never be proved?"

He rose and opened the window. The odour of damp earth and withered leaves came in with the wind. Small moths appeared out of the darkness and fluttered round the lamp.

"And do you think that that evening, while you were sitting here in this room . . . do you think that Eugen Bischoff in the pavilion saw the same visions?" I asked.

Dr Gorski turned and walked away from the window.

"What do you mean, the same?" he said. "The answer is no. The dreadful visions you saw came from your unconscious. Leprosy, for instance. You have several times been to the East, you have travelled in east Asia. Did you never even once feel, perhaps hardly consciously, a slight fear of that most terrible scourge of Asia? Think about it, baron. Eugen Bischoff? For years he had had one great fear: fear of losing Dina, of losing her to you. And in that unhappy hour he had a dreadful vision of her in your arms. What happened next? The shot, the first shot that hit the wall, may give us a clue. That shot was meant for you, baron. He may then have been seized with horror at what he had done, and turned the weapon against himself. When you walked into the room – do you remember his expression when he saw you? He saw you standing there alive, though he had shot you in the heart. It was with a feeling of infinite astonishment that Eugen Bischoff passed into the next world."

"And Solgrub?" Felix asked from the window.

"Solgrub was an officer in the Russian army, he took part in the Manchurian campaign. What do any of us really know about others? Each of us has his own Day of Judgment inside himself. Who knows? Perhaps it was the dead in that campaign who in his last hour rose against him."

He went over to the table and swept some dust from the cover of the old book.

"There the monster lies," he said. "It will do no more mischief, its time has passed. Through how many hands may it have passed in the course of the centuries? Would you like to keep it, Felix? If not, I have all sorts of mouldering learned junk at home, I feel well in the odour of yellowing parchment. The pages that are written on are yours, baron. Keep them in memory of a time when I saw you as I never again want to see a human being."

When I left the house Dina was standing by the garden gate. I had to pass her, there was no other way out. Deep, burning pain rose in me, I thought of what had been and could never be again, there were shades between us. For a moment her hand lay in mine, and then it vanished in the dark. I raised my hat. Silently we went our separate ways.

Editor's Postscript

When the Great War broke out Gottfried Adalbert Baron von Yosch and Klettenfeld rejoined the army as a volunteer. He was sent to the front, and was killed some months later while on a mounted reconnaissance patrol in the wooded country of Kostelniece during the battle of Limanova. His account of the events of the autumn of 1909 was found with other papers in the saddle-bag of his horse.

During the long Russian nights of December 1914 the novel – Baron von Yosch's posthumous work can hardly be properly described as anything else – was passed from hand to hand by the officers of the 6th Royal and Imperial Regiment of Dragoons. I received it from my squadron commander – without any comment – towards the end of the month. The reasons why the baron had resigned his commission five years before the outbreak of war were known to most of us. The suicide of the court actor Bischoff caused a considerable stir, and I well remember the part played in that affair by Baron von Yosch.

I expected, when I began looking through his papers, to find an attempt at self-justification, a perhaps embellished but essentially truthful account of the facts of the case. So far as purely external events are concerned, the first part of his story in fact corresponds with the real course of events. This made it the more surprising when I discovered that from a certain point onwards the story loses all contact with reality. At that point (it occurs in Chapter 8 where the author characteristically states: "Inside me and all round me everything had changed, and I had returned to the world of reality") the story takes a sharp turn into fantasy. Should it be necessary to state explicitly that Baron von Yosch caused the suicide of the court actor Bischoff, a man with a tendency to depression who was therefore easily influenced, and that, when he was called to account by the dead man's relatives and was driven into a corner, he took refuge in telling a lie on his word of honour? That is the truth of the matter. Everything else, the intervention of the engineer, the hunt for the "monster", the mysterious concoction, the vision, is hazardous invention. In reality the affair, which was reported to His Majesty's Chancery, ended in Baron von Yosch's being found guilty by a court of honour.

What was Baron von Yosch's purpose in writing this story? Did he intend to publish it? Did he hope that the court of honour would revise its verdict? That strikes me as highly improbable. Not all his intellectual faculties were equally developed, but he was by no means deficient in a sense of reality. But if his story was not intended for publication, why the very substantial effort entailed in telling it, which must have taken up years of his life?

Experienced criminologists provide the answer. They point to the "play with the evidence", the self-tormenting urge, observable in many of those found guilty by the courts, to force a new interpretation on the evidence of their crime, to prove to themselves that they might have been acquitted if fate had not decided against them.

Was it revolt against unalterable fate? But – looked at from a higher standpoint – has this not always been the origin of all art? Does not every eternal masterpiece derive from the experience of disgrace, humiliation, wounded pride? The thoughtless mob may wildly applaud a work of art – to me it reveals the devastated mind of its creator. In all the great symphonies of tones, colours and ideas I see a gleam of the marvellous colour trumpet red, a faint reflection of the great vision that for a short while raised the Master above the bewildering maze of his tormenting guilt.

In conclusion let me state that I succeeded in overcoming Baron von Yosch's closest relatives' reservations about publishing his story. Publication takes place with their consent.